Thomas Bernhard

# Gargoyles

Thomas Bernhard was born in Holland in 1931 and grew up in Austria. He studied music at the Universität Mozarteum in Salzburg. In 1957 he began a second career as a playwright, poet, and novelist. The winner of the three most distinguished and coveted literary prizes awarded in Germany, he has become one of the most widely translated and admired writers of his generation. His novels published in English include *The Loser*, *The Lime Works*, *Correction*, *Concrete*, *Woodcutters*, and *Wittgenstein's Nephew*; a number of his plays have been produced off-Broadway, at the Guthrie Theater in Minneapolis, and at theaters in London and throughout Europe. The five segments of his memoir were published in one volume, *Gathering Evidence*, in 1985. Thomas Bernhard died in 1989.

# GARGOYLES

# GARGOYLES

## THOMAS BERNHARD

*Translated from the German by*

RICHARD AND CLARA WINSTON

*Vintage International*
VINTAGE BOOKS
A DIVISION OF RANDOM HOUSE, INC.
NEW YORK

FIRST VINTAGE INTERNATIONAL EDITION, OCTOBER 2006

The Library of Congress has cataloged the Knopf edition as follows:
Bernhard, Thomas.
[Verstörung. English]
Gargoyles. Translated from the German by Richard and Clara Winston.—
1st American ed.
p.  cm.
PZ4.B5248 Gar PT2662.E7
833'.9'14    70106630

Vintage ISBN-10: 1-4000-7755-9
Vintage ISBN-13: 978-1-4000-7755-7

www.vintagebooks.com

146086900

*The eternal silence of these infinite spaces terrifies me.*

# GARGOYLES

ON the twenty-sixth my father drove off to Salla at two o'clock in the morning to see to a schoolteacher whom he found dying and left dead. From there he set out toward Hüllberg to treat a child who had fallen into a hog tub full of boiling water that spring. Discharged from the hospital weeks ago, it was now back with its parents.

He liked seeing the child, and dropped by there whenever he could. The parents were simple people, the father a miner in Köflach, the mother a servant in a butcher's household in Voitsberg. But the child was not left alone all day; it was in the care of one of the mother's sisters. On this day my father described the child to me in greater detail than ever before, adding that he was afraid it had only a short time to live. "I can say for a certainty that it won't last through the winter, so I am going to see it as often as possible now," he said. It struck me that he spoke of the child as a beloved person, very quietly and without having to consider his words. He let himself express a natural affection for the child as he hinted at the surroundings in which the child had grown up, not so much reared as guarded by its parents, and explained his speculations about these parents and their relationship to the child by filling out the details of the environment. While he spoke, he paced back and forth in his room, and soon no longer had the slightest need to lie down again.

My father was the only doctor in a relatively large and "difficult" district, now that the other doctor had moved to Graz, where he had accepted a teaching post at the university. "The chance of a replacement," my father said, "is practically nil. A man would be mad to want to start a practice here." For his own part, he said, he was used to sacrificing himself to a sick populace given to violence as well as insanity. My being home for the weekend was a tranquilizer for him, he said, and one that was more and more necessary. He seemed tired. But when I threw open the shutters and the light from the Ache river dazzled us, he said he would take a walk. "Come," he said, "come along." While I was dressing, he talked about a "phenomenon of nature," a chestnut tree that had burst into blossom now, at the end of September. He had discovered it by the riverside beyond the village. This would be a good opportunity, he said, for us to discuss something he had long wanted to talk about. Probably, I thought, something connected with my studies in Leoben, something to do with mining. This was the right time for it, he said, before he was taken up with the day's quota of patients. "You know," he said, "often it's all too much for me."

We did not want to wake my sister, and went out to the vestibule for our coats as quietly as possible. But as we were about to leave the house, the bell rang. At the door stood someone I did not know, who turned out to be an innkeeper from Gradenberg. He asked my father to come with him at once.

And so we rode to Gradenberg in the innkeeper's wagon instead of strolling along the Ache and having our discussion. There was no more talk about the flowering chestnut tree. Instead we heard a most unsettling tale about the innkeeper's wife.

She had been busy until two o'clock in the morning, her husband said, serving miners who had already been drunk for several hours and had divided into two hostile groups. Suddenly one of the miners without the slightest provocation struck her on the head, and she had dropped unconscious to the floor. The horrified miners carried her up to the bedroom on the second floor of the inn, her head bumping several times against the banister, and deposited her on her bed. Her husband woke up when the miners opened the bedroom door, and listened, dazed from sleep, to an account of the incident. The suddenly sobered miners wanted him to go to the police and lodge a complaint at once, that very night, against the assailant, a man named Grössl, who had run off but whom they all could identify. The police, including the constable supposedly on duty, had all been asleep, the innkeeper said. But by showering the police station windows with pebbles he had finally roused someone and been admitted. At first the police had advised him to come back in the forenoon to make a statement for the record, but he had insisted that the statement be recorded right then and there, and demanded that some of the constables at least come to the inn with him because his wife was lying there unconscious, the miners were still waiting, and he felt that they, too, should present their statements without delay. But the whole thing had taken too long; by the time he returned to the inn with two of the constables, all the miners except one were gone. His first thought was that he should not have left his wife alone for a moment, for as he entered the bedroom and saw the miner Kolig, who had been there all this time, the most horrible suspicions and imaginings ran through his mind. He did not know the man at all well, was acquainted with him merely from his occasional visits to the inn, and did not regard him as a neighbor in the sense of his being trustworthy. Moreover the miner spoke a Styrian dialect unpleasantly different from the dialect of the vicinity.

Albert Kolig was so drunk that though still on his feet he could not speak even the shortest sentence. The younger of the constables promptly told him to sit down in the armchair in the corner and began questioning him, while the other constable took pictures of the woman lying on the bed as motionless as if she were a corpse. The answers Kolig gave for the record were in fact useless. He could not sit up and was on the point of keeling over when the constable, losing patience, pulled him up and yanked and shoved him out into the hall.

The culprit, Grössl, was reputed to be the kind of man who the moment he entered a tavern was bound to stay until he had made some kind of ruckus. The constables said that it would not be difficult to find him and in view of his previous convictions the chances were that he would be in for a sentence of several years, since the facts of the case were plain enough: The blow on the woman's head had evidently caused a severe injury, for otherwise she would not be still unconscious. As soon as the older constable spoke the words "severe injury," everyone realized that a doctor would have to be called. "Meanwhile several hours have passed," the innkeeper said.

It was already half past four when we arrived in Gradenberg. The innkeeper led us up to the bedroom, where the two constables were standing. My father had all of us go out into the hall. While he was examining the woman—in my brief glimpse of her I had the impression that she had given up the ghost—the two constables in the corridor discussed Kolig, who lay in a drunken stupor on the floor. They said he was dimwitted and was treating his family of six more and more vilely. They did not know what to do with him. When my father emerged from the bedroom, they dragged Kolig away from the stairs, which he had half blocked with his legs. Then they paid no more attention to him.

The woman was in fact seriously injured and had to be taken to the Köflach hospital at once, my father said. He asked the constables to carry her carefully downstairs and place her in the rack wagon.

The constables carried the innkeeper's wife out of the damp room with its green and brown wallpaper and cheap pine furniture, a room that must have been gloomy even on the brightest day. As the constables cautiously descended the steps with their charge, my father looked at me and then past me, and I thought that his look boded very ill for the inn-keeper's wife.

While I took my seat in the wagon beside the innkeeper, who drove, my father sat behind us next to the patient.

During the whole ride, which we shortened by cutting across Krennhof, the innkeeper and I did not exchange a word. Because of the early hour the drive went quickly and easily. I had not been in this vicinity for a long time, I realized. I had to think far back to my earliest childhood to catch a glimpse of myself here and there playing by Gradner Brook. It struck me how seldom I had accompanied my father on his rounds, and that ever since my mother's death I had been left entirely to myself. It is the same for my sister, who must be feeling it even more painfully than I.

In keeping with our mood, I imagine, the innkeeper, who had talked so much on the way to Gradenberg, did not say a word on the way to Köflach. It would hardly have been fitting for me to strike up any conversation with him. If I had understood my father right, there was little hope that the woman would survive the ride to Köflach. But when the hospital attendants lifted her out of the wagon, she was not yet dead. She died, however, while we were still in the hospital, before she could be brought into the only operating room, and her husband sensed the moment of her passing. While the attendants were wheeling her down the corridor, he had held her hand and wept. They did not let him stay with the body, but led him down to the courtyard where, left entirely to himself, he had to wait half an hour for my father. I let him alone, but unobtrusively kept watch over him. Then my father came down and walked about the yard with him, trying to calm him. He spoke to the innkeeper of the things that had to be done now, about arranging the funeral, the inquest, filing a charge against Grössl for manslaughter. It would be wise for him to stay around people now, my father said, not to isolate himself in his anguish, withdraw into his pain. My father said he would take care of certain necessary errands, like going to court, and would accompany him on others to ease his grief, first of all to see his wife who was being moved to the autopsy room.

My father said that he had diagnosed a cerebral hemorrhage, which would have been fatal in any case. He would be receiving the exact details of the autopsy from the district coroner later in the morning. It was of no importance that the innkeeper had not notified him of the fatal blow until three hours after the incident, my father said. The woman could not have been saved. The deceased woman was thirty-three, and my father had known her for years. It had always seemed to him that innkeepers treated their wives with extreme callousness, he said. They themselves usually went to bed early, having overworked themselves all day on their slaughtering, their cattle dealing, their farms. But because they thought of nothing but the business, they left their wives to take care of the taverns until the early morning hours, exposed to the male clients who drank steadily so that as the night wore on their natural brutality became less and less restrained. My father said this to me in an interval when we fell a bit behind the innkeeper, who was walking with us but seemed in a total daze. "All these long drinking bouts end badly," my father said. "And in this region a high percentage of them end in a fatality. The innkeepers' own wives are often the victims; the innkeepers set these helpless women to tending the public rooms so they can extract every penny from their drunken patrons by pouring the cheapest brandy into their unresisting guts."

When we had caught up to the innkeeper again, my father assured him that it would be easy to find Grössl now that the police were informed of it all. No matter where he was holed up, Grössl would not be able to stay hidden long. The innkeeper's tears and distraught air were affecting precisely because his dealings with cattle and the tavern world had made him the embodiment of the district's characteristic brutality. But the more my father tried to talk to him, the more pointless the effort seemed. Finally my father contented himself with giving the man the necessary instructions in what I thought a very simple and easily understood way. Then we left him to himself again.

My father went to the autopsy room and talked with the coroner and his assistants. Meanwhile I kept an eye on the innkeeper as he sat on the single bench in the hospital yard. I guessed that his wife's body was in the two-wheeled morgue cart that a young attendant pushed past me. The sight of the morgue cart was nothing new to me, for my way to school had led past the hospital and I often used to pause at the spot where the morgue could be seen between two elderberry bushes so I could look at the cart that stood by the entrance to the morgue day and night when it was not in use. It was housed in an open shed on the side of the building visible to me. This sheet-metal morgue cart had always had a macabre fascination for me, and often appeared as a major, horrible prop on the stage of my childhood dreams. The young attendant, barely past school age, pushed the cart to the entrance of the morgue, and I heard my father coming from that direction. We went out of the hospital yard, moving quickly along the walls so as to keep out of sight of the innkeeper, who was still sitting on the bench. My father, I thought, wherever he feels at home, which is with patients and in hospitals, doesn't act as if he were part of a vast, opaque business organization, though that's what people accuse doctors of nowadays, but rather as I've seen him act today, as if he were part of a more and more crystal-clear science. I suppose there are many doctors like some I have met who are nothing but businessmen, and talk and act like businessmen even when they have keen scientific minds. But my father isn't one of them.

"You see nothing but sad sights when you come along

with me," my father said. "That's why I hesitate most of the
time to have you come along on my calls, because it turns out
that everyone I have to visit and touch and treat proves to be
sick and sad." No matter what the trouble was, he went on,
he was continually moving about in a sick world among sick
people, sick individuals; and even though this world might
claim, might even pretend, to be healthy, it was still sick and
the people, the individuals, were always sick, even the so-
called healthy ones. "I'm accustomed to that, but it might
possibly upset you, might give you harmful thoughts. I've
noticed you tend to be upset by everything and everyone, to
think about everything and everyone in a harmful way." And
my sister did the same, to an even more dangerous extent, he
went on. "But it would be wrong to refuse to face the fact
that everything is *fundamentally sick and sad*"—those were
his very words—and for that reason he was now and again
"tempted" to take me or my sister along on his sick-calls.
"It's always a risk," he said. Most of all, he added, he was
afraid that one of us, my sister or I, could be harmed for life
by seeing a patient and his illness, whereas he meant it to
have just the opposite effect.

We went on into Köflach. He wanted to go to the bank
and the post office, but they were still closed, and so he took
me along to a lawyer friend of his who had been a fellow
student at the university in Graz. I knew the man from his
summer visits to us. He was a successful lawyer specializing
in real estate. My father was hoping his friend would provide
us with breakfast.

We rang. The door was opened, and we entered an apart-
ment that was furnished opulently by the standards of a
small town and at first glance had a very cosy look about it,

although the individual pieces were not especially tasteful. The first thing you noticed was the many chairs and couches. The lawyer's young wife received us and at once ushered us into the dining room. Before long the lawyer himself appeared. My father said he had only a little time; he had to return home with me. During the breakfast, for which we had arrived just in time and which was more lavish than any I have ever eaten, I sat where I could look down into the street and watch what was going on there as we talked about Grössl's murder of the innkeeper's wife. My father remarked that it was horrible how people went at each other without knowing why, especially in the taverns, as soon as they lost their ordinary inhibitions. He was sure, he said, that this fellow Grössl did not know why he had knocked down the innkeeper's wife. "It may be," my father said, "that he doesn't even know that he killed her." Nowadays, he went on, the country people who first degenerate into brutality and then into total helplessness about their brutality, who degenerate in all respects and cannot help themselves, are alarmingly in the majority.

The fact was, he continued, that there are more brutal and criminal types in the country than in the city. "Brutality, like violence, is the very fundament of life in the country. Brutality in the city is nothing compared to the brutality in the country, and the violence in the city is nothing compared to the violence of the country. Crime in the city, urban crime, is nothing compared to crime in the country, rural crime. In fact urban crimes are ridiculous compared to the country kind."

The innkeeper, he declared, was a born criminal, born to violence. He remained a cattle dealer every moment and in all life situations. "Even though he's crying now," my father said, "it's livestock he's really crying over. For an innkeeper his wife is nothing but livestock. One day he claps a brutish hand on her and draws her out of the undifferentiated herd of unwed girls and breaks her to his use. An inn like that, like every butcher's or cattle dealer's or peasant's house in this area, is a brutal prison for women. If you keep your ears open, whenever you go about the countryside you hear the women inside their houses crying because their men have beaten them. As I go about, there is hardly a man I see who isn't repulsive. When I enter one of these houses, I enter an atmosphere of brutality, of violence; I am forever carrying my doctor's bag into a world of criminals. The people who live under the Glein Alp and under the Kor Alp and in the Kainach and Gröbnitz valleys are perfect specimens of a Styria that for thousands and millions of years has been built on the basest kind of physical abuse."

But then my father recalled his early visits to the miner's child in Hüllberg. He described how he was received cordially and bidden good-by just as graciously after he had spent a quarter of an hour there, calmed and reassured. But this did not mean that what he had said about people like the innkeeper applied solely to the more prosperous natives. The Hüllberg parents and their child were exceptional. On the whole "the poor are twice as brutal, base and criminal as anyone else, and the pressures on them to make them so are far greater."

My father did not speak about the schoolteacher who had been the object of his first call that day—did not speak of him, I thought, because the man had died too soon under his hands, before he could have any idea of him. I thought that the teacher had already been forgotten, for after my father talked about the child and its burns once more, and gave a description of the child's manner of speech, he reverted to the subject of the innkeeper. The innkeeper was waiting for us in the hospital, my father said, and would have to drive us back to Gradenberg in his wagon before going home. Now he was probably in the morgue. My father had meant to go in with him, but it must have slipped his mind. I imagined that right now the attendants in the morgue were giving the innkeeper his dead wife's clothing, and sure enough the innkeeper was actually waiting for us, with the woman's clothes bundled under his arm, at the hospital entrance after we had left the lawyer's and quickly been to the post office and the bank.

On the way back to Gradenberg my father went over the patients he still had to visit in the course of the day. He mentioned the names Saurau, Ebenhöh, Fochler, and Krainer. Whereas I had already been strongly affected by the things I had experienced in connection with the death of the innkeeper's wife, my father now no longer showed the slightest fatigue. Sitting beside the innkeeper, who drove the wagon as calmly as if nothing had happened, the two of us pictured, each for himself, the patients still to be visited. Outside Krennhof the innkeeper stopped at a butcher's and, apologizing, got out to arrange some business matter. While he was gone for a few minutes, my father commented that he had known this fellow from childhood, that only ten years ago he had been still a young man, but now was steadily putting on fat, walked in a disgustingly bowlegged manner of increasing sexual clumsiness, and had become altogether obnoxious. As for the innkeeper's wife, my father said, each time he visited Gradenberg he had found the woman equally repulsive. When such people had no children, the meaning gradually drained out of their marriage so that it degenerated into something perverse and vicious that was destined to end in abject misery unless some accident, such as this man Grössl's running amuck, put a stop to it.

Along the last stretch of the road we had to turn to avoid a herd of cattle. At this point the innkeeper spoke up, saying several times that he had not yet grasped what had happened; it was still unreal to him.

When we reached Gradenberg, we saw a crowd gathered in front of the inn. The judicial commission had just arrived on the scene. As I got down from the wagon, I noticed curiosity-seekers all over the place, some standing nearby, some at a remove.

My father told me to wait in front of the inn. He strode rapidly inside to confer with the judicial commission, whose members were assembled in the public room. The inn was filled from top to bottom with officials who were murmuring steadily among themselves. In an open window on the second floor, the bedroom window, I noticed the heads of two constables. I paced back and forth in front of the inn until my father came out with the innkeeper, who was to drive us home. All the miners who had witnessed the killing had been summoned to testify. It was Saturday; the mine was closed. Most of them could no longer reconstruct the incident; they made contradictory statements; but two of them had *seen* Grössl when he knocked the innkeeper's wife down. That was enough for them. Despite my father's prediction, Grössl was still at large. Probably, my father said, he was hiding somewhere in the immediate vicinity. Everyone thought it unlikely that he could escape to any great distance, even though he had enough money to have even fled the country.

Back home, we got into our car at once. "We're driving to Stiwoll," my father said.

The road from Graden to Kainach was blocked, partly on account of Grössl. But since we were recognized, we were allowed to pass. A case like Grössl's was naturally a sensation, and the whole region was agog. Everyone was excited by the death of the innkeeper's wife. The news had spread rapidly through the constabulary headquarters, as we noticed especially in Afling, where we stopped at my uncle's. My father had brought medicines for my uncle's wife. We entered the house and called, went down to the lower rooms and into the kitchen, and found that there was not a soul in the unlocked house. My father deposited the medicines on the kitchen cupboard, left a note, and we took our leave.

A year before my mother's death, my father said, he had been in Afling with her, at the funeral of one of his old classmates, and she had talked constantly about her own impending death. Whereas *he* had as yet discovered no signs of her fatal disease, *she* was already *permeated* by it; that was something he realized only much later. After that visit in Afling he had observed a mysterious and total transformation in her, which baffled him as a physician. There was an increasing melancholia that gradually infected all of us. He recalled every one of the things she had said, could see the road they had walked on before and after the funeral. It had been this time of year, the end of September. Everything connected with that funeral in Afling was still remarkably distinct to him. Especially on fair days, when the air has a particular transparency and nature is lovely for its tranquility alone, one sorrows for the dead with redoubled force.

The essential elements of a person, my father said, come to light only when we must regard him as lost to us, when everything he has done seems to have been a taking leave of us. Suddenly the true nature of everything about him that was merely preparation for his ultimate death becomes truly visible.

All through the drive through the Söding Valley my father talked about my mother. His reveries centered on her, he said, rather than his dreams. Her presence often steadied and encouraged him during periods that seemed outwardly to be fully taken up by his medical work. As a result he had been able to reach a clear view of death as a fact of nature. Now he understood her, who had lived beside him so many years and been loved but never understood. You were never truly together with one you loved until the person in question was dead and actually inside you.

From the day of the funeral in Afling, my father continued, she had often asked him to take her along on his calls. Nowadays this desire on her part no longer seemed so incomprehensible. In the nature of things it had not been possible for her to *study* the suffering and torment of the world, but from the day of the funeral in Afling on, this subject was constantly on her mind. During this period he had often spoken with her about us children, above all about the difficulty of channeling parental affection into educational lines. But she used often to say to him that we seemed to her more the children of the landscape around us than of our parents. Holding this view, she had felt us, my sister to an even greater degree than myself, to be creatures sprung entirely from nature, for which reason we had always remained alien to her. Because the three of us were completely helpless after her death, my father said, and my sister and I were in the most dangerous phase of development, she twelve and I sixteen years old, he had thought of remarrying. "In fact the thought came to me during the funeral itself," my father said when we were already in sight of Stiwoll. But the idea had been more and more repressed *by our mother inside him*.

As he said this, I remembered the letter I had written to him a few days ago, in which I had tried to sketch the uneasy relationship among us three, between him and me and between him and my sister and between me and my sister. I had written to him fancying that I would receive an answer, and now I realized that no such answer would ever be forthcoming.

My father will never be able to answer the questions I asked him in that letter.

Our relationship is difficult through and through, in fact chaotic, and the relationship between him and my sister and between me and my sister is the most difficult, the most chaotic of all.

In the letter I had tried to define certain things about our relationship by citing seemingly simple but to me extremely important details. In the writing I had taken the greatest pains not to offend my father. Nor to offend anybody. From my years of observation I found it fairly easy to sketch a picture of us that could be considered truthful from all three sides. My letter had been composed very calmly; I did not allow myself to show any excitement, although I did not evade the central matters that concerned me, such central matters, posed as indirect or direct questions, as for example who was to blame for my sister's most recent attempt at suicide, or for my mother's early death. I had long wanted to write such a letter and had started on it repeatedly, but had each time been overcome by doubts about the usefulness of this sort of accounting. It had always been impossible for me to write to him. Each time I would immediately become aware of the awkwardness of suddenly expressing in black and white things that for years had only been private thoughts, speculations. Then too I was checked by a reluctance to bring up possibly long-forgotten matters as essential evidence for my view of us. For I would have had to proceed with sincerity and therefore ruthlessness, and yet show consideration for all concerned. That, too, made such a letter impossible for such a long time.

But on the previous Monday it had suddenly become easy for me to write the letter. In a single draft of only eight pages I set forth my analysis of the whole complex, which culminated in questions of whether there was any way to clarify the condition we were all in, and whether our relations could be improved. When I was done, I looked the text over several times and found nothing that should dissuade me from mailing it. My father must surely have received the letter by Tuesday morning. But up to now he had not so much as mentioned the matter, although it was apparent from his whole manner that he had not only received the letter punctually, but had also read and studied it with the greatest attention and had not forgotten it.

In Stiwoll, too, as I saw the moment we drove into town, my father was very well known.

Thanks to his excellent memory, he could address everybody he met by name. He also knew the situation of every individual.

Whenever he felt that I needed some pertinent information about someone with whom he had exchanged a greeting or a few words, he gave me a brief characterization.

We walked rapidly through the town to visit a certain Bloch, a dealer in real estate. He liked the man, my father said. Married to a woman of fifty, his own age, the realtor voluntarily stayed on in this dull mountain community, whose natives were by nature hostile to him, and found his consolation in the pleasures of his business.

There was another doctor in Stiwoll, my father said. But Bloch had relieved this doctor of the lasting shame of having to treat a Jew, which Bloch was, by consulting my father. Bloch's father had also lived in Stiwoll.

Between Bloch and my father, despite the distance of fifteen miles and the intervening high mountains, there had developed a friendship that had, as my father put it, "something philosophical about it." Bloch, he said, occupied the house that had been his father's, who had been killed by the Germans.

As I saw at once, this was one of the finest houses in Stiwoll, on the right side of the street that led from the main square. The façade itself pleased me precisely because it looked so neglected, gray in keeping with its actual age, and also rather battered from the last war. As we entered the freshly plastered vaulted hall, I instantly decided that Bloch had good taste.

He would visit Bloch at least once a week for a longish talk, my father said, a discussion that he or Bloch took turns at leading. I might find it hard to believe, my father said, considering the general tenor of things in Stiwoll, but the two of them conducted "autopsies on the body of nature" as well as "on the body of the world and its history." They discussed "comparative political science, applied natural history, literary criticism," and dealt "unsparingly with society and the state." But in general the main theme in Bloch's house was politics, and they tended to talk about people more in regard to their political than their private beings. Meeting in a first-floor study, they conducted an analysis of the world on the most stringent intellectual principles, and left no margin for any illusions whatsoever. Most of the time the arts were rather scanted, my father said, but occasionally they would turn to them out of courtesy to Bloch's wife.

Bloch was sitting in an office to the right of the vestibule, separated from it only by a glass partition, and dictating with obvious excitement to his secretary. As he later mentioned, he was addressing a letter to the Voitsberg surveyor, whom I also knew. My father tapped on the office window, and Bloch came out. He greeted us pleasantly and led us at once into the study on the second floor. The fact is that nowhere in a rural area have I ever seen so many books all together as in Bloch's library. Moreover, as I observed, they were all well used, and were not here for their so-called bibliophilic value, which people in German-speaking countries set such ridiculous store by—aside from a Latin edition of the Nuremberg physician Schedel's world history, of which there are only a few copies in the whole world.

Bloch asked what had brought my father to Stiwoll at this unusual morning hour. My father said he wanted to return Kant's *Prolegomena* and Marx's *Dissertation,* both of which he had finished. He took the two volumes out of his medical bag and put them down on the table. Then he mentioned the books he would like to borrow: Nietzsche's lectures *On the Future of Our Educational Institutions*, a French edition of Pascal's *Pensées*, and Diderot's *Mystification*. He had to call on a woman named Ebenhöh on Piberweg, he said. Bloch did not know her.

Since he had nothing else in the house, Bloch poured us glasses of white wine, Klöscher. Early that morning, he said, he had again suffered from one of his "frightful" headaches, but it had vanished after he began working intensively on his business correspondence. He was taking more and more of the headache remedy my father had prescribed for him, he said. And he had not slept the past four or five days. My father warned him against overdoing it with the medicine, which was dangerous to the kidneys.

Recently, Bloch said, he had managed to buy a sizable property in the vicinity of Semriach. "It took me two years to put over the deal," he said. A week earlier it had been plowland, but he saw it as a prime building parcel that could be divided into more than a hundred lots. That way he would be able to dispose of the property quickly. "You have to be able to wait it out," he said. This was his biggest deal of the year, he added. He asked for a better sedative; my father wrote a prescription. *"Naturally* I'm not liked," Bloch said, and my father stood up. They arranged to meet the next Wednesday. For the past two years my father had been seeing Bloch every Wednesday.

We went to Frau Ebenhöh on foot.

"Bloch has the art of seeing his life as an easily understood mechanism that he can keep regulated, speed up or slow down, according to his needs," my father said. "However he uses his powers, the result is always practically useful, which makes the whole thing bearable. He finds pleasure in this art and is always trying to teach it to his family." Basically, my father said, Bloch was the only person he could talk with in a manner that was never awkward, and also the only person whom he wholly trusted. Bloch had become a friend who meant more than other lost friends, all those others scattered throughout the countryside pretending to be its intelligentsia, exiled in deep, sunless valleys, in small towns and dull marketplaces and villages, accepting their monotonous fate as country doctors in a way that used to pain him when he himself was still a student, but now only repelled him. For all these people, the high point had been their university years, he said. Once discharged into a world disastrously trustful of them, they fell into a horrible familial and consulting-room apathy, irrespective of whether they worked in hospitals or in private practice. He was shocked, my father said, by the total submergence of these former classmates, as he discovered whenever he wrote to one or another of them, letters he felt to be increasingly pointless. Lifelong dilettantes, they married much too soon or much too late and were destroyed by their increasing lack of ideas, lack of imagination, lack of strength, and finally by their wives. "I met Bloch just at the moment when I had no friends left, nothing but correspondents connected with me by a shared youth and the shared trustfulness of the world toward us."

Now and then, my father said, he would see one or another of them who in the meantime had become totally absorbed in the sexual pecking-order. Such a colleague would sentimentalize about friendship. But these encounters took place nowadays only by chance, at railroad stations or conventions, and he would feel nauseated, my father said, and have to keep a tight grip on himself so as not to show his feelings. At the university and in their period of internship, they used to talk a great deal about research, about the overwhelming sickness of humanity, about discoveries, about making maximal intellectual efforts, about medical science, the pitiable condition of man and the necessity for taking an uncompromising stand. But all that was left of them were well-dressed quacks who traveled much, hurriedly said hello when they ran into each other, and talked about their family problems, about the houses they were building, and obsessively about their cars. Bloch, on the other hand, was a man who did not lose his grip in spite of the wild way history was accelerating its pace, by the hundredfold or thousandfold from year to year.

From Stiwoll, in the midst of a rooted, by now grotesque anti-Semitism, among the coarse mountaineers who despised him and did business with him, Bloch had a better view of the world than men in metropolitan centers. Stiwoll was for him a kind of "gruesome private hell in the mountains" that he had created for himself ten years ago. He had many friends here and there throughout the world, though few relations, who shook their heads over him in astonishment or disapproval. From time to time he declared that he stayed on in Stiwoll to engage in open-ended studies for the benefit of his own people.

My father said that he was looking forward to Diderot's *Mystification,* that belatedly discovered essay Bloch had recommended to him. He was more and more turning to the French writers nowadays, he said, and away from the Germans. "Basically I've never really had much need for pure literature, and this tendency of mine seems to be growing stronger. The closer I come to clarity and logic, the less receptive I find myself to so-called belles-lettres." He regarded writing of that kind, he said, as an annoying and on the whole ridiculous falsification of nature. Writers were always soiling nature, whether they were more or less unknowns or more or less celebrated, and whether they put current events in the foreground or background.

"You could not have noticed in the short time we were there," my father said, "but except for the most extraordinary works Bloch has no entertainment literature in his library." He had the impulse to visit Bloch in Stiwoll more often than once a week, he said, but recognized that he must not strain the relationship.

I was struck by the strength of the affection, otherwise rare in him, that my father showed for this real estate man Bloch. Perhaps he was carrying it too far, without Bloch's himself being aware of this feeling on my father's part. But I also suddenly realized how alone my father is and how meagerly he opens his heart to us, his children.

He's almost never at home, I thought. My sister is always alone and he is always alone too.

Actually my father meets more and more people in order to be more and more alone.

But he must have sensed that I was giving thought to his almost total isolation. He hated to be an object of pity, and said: "I am exaggerating. It's very different from what you think. Everything is always very different. Communication is impossible."

Our path to Frau Ebenhöh's led through an unfenced orchard whose fallen apples and pears had not been gathered, as I at once noticed. The irregularities in the orchard and garden were suspect, suggesting a person whose inner rhythms were disturbed; the quietude of the garden was of a feverish, morbid kind. All the windows of the one-story house were open. It was sultry. Behind one of those windows lies Frau Ebenhöh, I thought.

I imagined her lying awake and listening for footsteps in the garden, deciding who it was by the sound of the footsteps. The sickroom proved to be exactly as I had imagined it, only gloomier. Her linens lay about everywhere, smelling of the fatal illness to which she was submitting without resistance.

I could see that someone had just been sitting in the large gray-green velvet upholstered easy chair near the sickbed. A neighbor woman? A relative? Whoever it was had been reading to her and had probably gone to the village to do some errand.

These houses are occupied by solitary old women who have been abandoned by their children and have restricted themselves to a minimal life. Entering such houses, I always feel close to suffocation. Flowers by the window in a long-necked glass vase; canary in a cage, eating and chirping heedlessly.

Underwear is no longer hidden, pain is no longer hidden, the sense of smell is dulled, there is no longer any reason to conceal frailties one is alone with.

My father simply walked into the bedroom. He woke the sleeping woman by rattling the birdcage with his stethoscope so that the flustered bird chirruped in alarm.

The smiles of such women who know they are done for and who wake from sleep to find that they are still in this painful world—these smiles are nothing but horror.

Now lying words are exchanged. My father speaks of the summery weather spreading over the entire countryside, of the colors everywhere. He has brought his son along, he says.

I approach the woman, moving into the gloom, then return to the easy chair. I pick up the book and sit down. *The Princess of Cleves,* I think, *The Princess of Cleves* in Stiwoll. I leaf through the book thinking: What kind of person is this patient lying here? Who was her husband?

All about the walls I notice large photographs of a bearded man, surely a schoolteacher; all the photographs show the same schoolteacher's face emerging from a huge beard.

Then my father alludes to her husband the schoolteacher, and talks about the change in weather and what a pity that people cannot make use of this change in weather, because it has come too late.

He talks about common acquaintances in Gratwein, in Übelbach, in Linz and Ligist. About a postmaster in Feistritz, a miller's wife in Wolfsberg. About a ghastly automobile accident.

Frau Ebenhöh talks about no longer having pain, about a teacher's wife from Unzmarkt who plays the church organ for her. She says that old pupils come to see her every day.

She points to the array of gifts on the table.

The priest visits her, she says. Her neighbor ("who's just gone to the village!") is reading to her, books she did not manage to read during her husband's lifetime. She often thinks about Oberwölz, where her sister, sick like herself, has been put into an old-age home. "Confined to her bed." She herself, Frau Ebenhöh, has always been opposed to the home, and whenever her son begins urging that she would be better taken care of in the Stiwoll old-age home, she begins to doubt her children's kindness. Her grandchildren always come to see her in Sunday clothes that need washing, and play with old newspapers in her room.

Her husband, she says, had been nominated as a socialist candidate for national deputy in 1948, but before the final election lists were posted he'd had his fatal accident, as my father knew.

She remembers that four of her husband's schoolmates carried the coffin. "All four are dead," she says. "Died in a short time, one after the other."

Only two months ago, when she came back from the hospital, everything had centered around fighting for sleep, she went on to say, but now it was a question of fighting to keep awake. The garden had come to a standstill. Nevertheless she had to complain of her neighbor: "Sometimes she doesn't turn up here for hours."

My father placed his stethoscope against her clothed chest and listened. He filled out a prescription. I noticed that he made an effort to stretch out the call, for all his eagerness to leave.

Frau Ebenhöh said that her life was a void without music, which she hadn't been able to play for such a long time now, only imagine ("You know, I can still hear it!"). And for the longest time it had seemed to her as if her body were already dead. "When I look in the mirror I fall into a terrible state."

She spoke of her sister, who was in the Oberwölz old-age home, sharing a room with six women her own age. She'd kept intending to visit her sister—that was before she imagined being sick herself. Now she would never see her again.

"Last night I dreamed I was standing under the Krimml

waterfall—that was one of my earliest childhood experiences —and calling for my mother again and again."

Suddenly she laughed.

She'd married her husband without knowing him, she said.

"Three weeks after I met him for the first time at the Corpus Christi procession in Köflach, he came from Stiwoll to fetch me—that was the evening before the wedding in Stiwoll and just the second time I'd seen him." She was the daughter of a sawmill foreman and had grown up on a hill just outside of Knittelfeld.

On the chest of drawers stood a plaster bust of Franz Schubert; the head had once broken at the neck and been glued. The bust stood on a pile of sheet music.

In her youth, Frau Ebenhöh said, she used to love to dance. At sixteen she had swum the length of the Mondsee in Upper Austria. For a long time she and her husband had made a hobby of studying Greek statuary. She'd been in Rome once, and once in Paris. They were both of thrifty habits and had managed to buy their own house in Stiwoll early in their marriage. Soon after the end of the First World War, they had come into some money, with which they had paid off the mortgage.

For fifteen years, she said, one of her brothers had been in the Stein Penitentiary—"a convict brother, a brother who's a criminal." Behind her husband's back she had sent him letters and money and packages every month. She did not speak about her brother's crime, but my father knows that he killed his fiancée. Upon his release from the penitentiary her brother had come to Stiwoll and lived in her house. She'd fixed a room for him in the attic, where he'd locked himself up from the moment he arrived and never went out. Three days after his release from Stein she had found him dead—he'd hanged himself from the window frame. His funeral had been so terribly sad, she said, she hadn't had the strength to go to it. And her husband had reproached her endlessly for having taken her brother in. That awful thing happening had made him feel uneasy in his own house, he used to say.

She had a photograph of her brother, taken the day he killed his fiancée and threw the body into the Mur below Fronleiten. She asked me to hand her an envelope lying on the table. I stood up and gave her the envelope, in which she kept the picture. "A handsome man," she said. For the remainder of our stay she went on holding the photograph in her hand. Looking down at the blanket, she described, in connection with her brother, her childhood years in Knittelfeld.

Never, not for a moment, had she ever thought of her brother as a bad person, she said.

My father must have had the feeling that this would be the last time he would be seeing Frau Ebenhöh, for otherwise he surely would have taken his departure.

"With closed eyes I see everything much more distinctly than I did then," she said.

"I have been thinking whom to leave my clothes to. They're in the wardrobe, all in good condition. . . . I made my house over to my son long ago, though I haven't let him know."

She could not say he was not concerned about her, she added, but he did no more than was his duty. Her daughter-in-law had always hated her. It had started as spontaneous dislike at their first meeting and had grown ever stronger over the years. "My son doesn't dare to love me any more because of the way his wife hates me." And by now, Frau Ebenhöh said, she was "crushed" by the more and more revolting stories her daughter-in-law concocted about her. The fact was that with her husband's death she had become all too vulnerable to the ill will of her son and her daughter-in-law. Her daughter-in-law had thrust her into the outer darkness of hopeless solitude, and her son had done nothing but look on. He'd entered into marriage much too soon; he'd been immature and regarded that girl from Köflach as a way to escape from his parents, and had gone downhill instantly. He was now employed as a helper to a tanner in Krottendorf, and worked even on Sundays. His clothes reeked when he came on a visit; they gave out a frightful odor of cadaver, and so did his wife's clothes and the grandchildren's clothes. Whenever they came, the whole house was filled with that odor of cadaver. After they left, she had to keep the windows open for hours or she couldn't bear it. But they themselves never noticed they smelled so awful.

Her son, she said, was "huge," with unusually long arms and "coarse" hands, but in the past he had always been good-natured. His father had been unhappy about the boy from the earliest years, for as soon as the child began to talk it became apparent that he'd never be very bright. And in fact his father had twice kept him back in his own elementary school. There'd never been any chance of his going to high school. Because of this son her husband had drifted more and more into a terrible depression. Tormented by doubts about the whole process of education, he'd found no peace, let alone any more satisfaction in his work. A psychiatrist he went to see in Graz did not help, merely cost a lot of money.

The two of them still kept hoping that the boy's sad condition, which cast a blight on both their lives, would end some day. But they had waited in vain for some sign of improvement. If her husband had not fallen to his death he would probably have been destroyed "slowly and miserably" by their son's feeble-mindedness, she thought. Then her son from one moment to the next, like an animal leaping up after crouching a long time, had suddenly gone after that Köflach girl, whose family went around with traveling exhibits to fairs and markets. He had to marry her because he made her pregnant right away.

At first her family had taken him along to the fairs in Styria, Lower Austria, and the Burgenland. But then, because that wasn't working out, his wife arranged for him to have that job with the Krottendorf tanner.

Frau Ebenhöh often imagined her son standing in the steaming tannery, stripped to the waist, dully stirring the vats with a wooden paddle, stirring hour after hour while his wife, "unwashed and undressed" in a "greasy housecoat," sat in her kitchen reading novels. She kept imagining her grandchildren's home getting more and more filthy and stinking, she said, and brooded over the riddle of how out of the union with a husband from such a good family she could have borne a son who increasingly seemed to her a beast. However far she went back in both families, her own as well as her husband's, she could see only "fine-nerved, decent people." Among them all her son stood alone, "a kind of monster." For her brother, the murderer, had also been one of the fine-nerved, kind, decent, intelligent, intellectually receptive, and she had never felt in the least ill at ease with him as she did with her own son. Granted, her son had never had any trouble with the law so far. Up to now his good nature had preserved him from crime. But she had been noticing more and more how her son's good nature was leaking away, giving way to a callousness that frightened her. There they were, her closest relatives, and when they came along talking all at once in their common way so that she could perfectly well hear them from her bed while they were still in the garden, tossing the word "grandmother" back and forth, it seemed to her as if they'd agreed on an infamous baseness directed against her. They let their children crawl around the floor, and sat down on the bed beside her, and it seemed to her she would suffocate. They grumbled about each other to her; her daughter-in-law called her son a dull-witted "big gut," and he called her a "lousy slut." When they had run through their stock of insults, they waited for the time they could leave again, the children in the lead once more, talking all at once in their common way, leaving that smell of cadaver behind.

She thought her son was going to sell her house after her death, Frau Ebenhöh said, and squander the money in no time at all. After all, he couldn't very well stay in Stiwoll. It made her sick to think of her furniture at the disposal of her son and her daughter-in-law—precious things like her piano, her husband's violin, which was on the chest of drawers, the folders of music, the books, all at the tender mercies of the heirs. She didn't have to go there to know in what a wretched, neglected state her son's family in Krottendorf lived. Once, when she was still well, they'd invited her to Krottendorf. She'd managed to avoid going by claiming she had a head cold; she'd been so afraid of facing in reality what she had been imagining for years. From Krottendorf that smell of cadaver spread far and wide, as far as Graz on days when the east wind was blowing. Anyone who lived in Krottendorf lived in the perpetual stench of a money-making inferno.

What always shocked her, she said, was the impassive way her son described his work in the tannery as monotonous, uninteresting, harmful to his lungs and kidneys. To be sure, the doctors who examined the three hundred Krottendorf tannery workers every two months had so far found nothing wrong with either his lungs or his kidneys. But after ten years of work in Krottendorf, Frau Ebenhöh said, peering out fixedly above her blanket as if looking all the way to Krottendorf, "after ten years of stirring those Krottendorf vats," changes took place in the lungs and kidneys of the workers. "Fatal ones," she said. "But my son has the toughest constitution you can imagine." His "gigantic" body had always seemed to her like something alien, to her just as much as to her husband. After finishing elementary school her son had stayed up in the attic where her brother had hanged himself, sitting torpidly in a chair day after day, staring into space, not saying a word, until her husband's accident. And right after his father's funeral, probably because this had been on his mind all along, he'd gone down to Knittelfeld, as she had mentioned, to the first skirt who came along, his wife. "The poor brute." She often thought that if he had stayed at home she might have saved him nevertheless. She had long felt sorry for him, in his dull helplessness, even though or perhaps because he was so senselessly and without any fault of his own ruining his parents' lives. But now she no longer felt sorry for him. She was sick of him. Now everything was ending for her in detestation of her own son and his wife and children.

And all the while she talked of her son, she told us, her mind dwelt on the thought that this room of hers was the one she was going to die in. It closed in on her at night, and she was afraid of suffocation. My father distracted her (and us) by talking about the Stub Alp. He described the stunted pines at the top, the cold autumnal air, the wind along the rocky peak, the rush of Lobming Brook down into the valley.

"I take my son with me more often nowadays," my father said. "He has to get to know people; that's going to be essential for him. . . . I live with my children but I can't see inside them any more than they can see inside me. The difficulties between parents and children are growing worse all the time. After a while there'll be no overcoming them, do what one will."

To this day he had not comprehended his wife's, my mother's, death. But then everything was always incomprehensible.

Who would have thought, only five years ago, that he would suddenly be *alone* with me and my sister.

"A good person whom everything depended on suddenly no longer exists," he said.

He knew I was doing all right at the Mining Academy in Leoben, he said. He wasn't worried about me, only about my sister. She was so susceptible to every illness, had such a withdrawn life, left to herself with our housekeeper most of the time. And she was so sensitive that some days she was simply incapable of leaving her room.

My father spoke very affectionately about us. Frau Ebenhöh seemed to be listening attentively to him.

He needs someone to listen to him now and then, I thought. I recalled Bloch.

But he rather imagined my sister and I could lean on each other when he was not around, he said.

My interest in the sciences made him happy, he said. He was *disturbed* by my taciturnity, not *alarmed,* because it wasn't morbid, just something I'd arrived at rationally. He thought my physical health was good.

"As far as I know his friends are all healthy young fellows, too," he said. "I enjoy seeing them whenever I'm in Leoben. I usually have dinner with my son in the Gärner Restaurant. But the worst of it is, I'm always in a hurry."

He was glad I had chosen my course of studies myself and was pushing on with them, to be finished as soon as possible. "He's making wonderful progress—he's better than all the others."

Leoben was a good place for studying mining engineering, not too big and not too small, a town that offered what was necessary and nothing superfluous, he said. The climate wasn't as good as up here at home, but still quite healthful. I took advantage of the amusements the town offered, but didn't go overboard. That above all reassured him. It seemed to him fantastic that I was all of twenty-one.

He rather wished I could go in somewhat more for sports, but I surely knew best what I ought to be doing. All in all, since he didn't scant me in any way, he could *expect* that I would act in good faith and fulfill his hopes. To do well always and everywhere took effort.

As for my sister, he'd been noticing things in her that were just like my mother, psychological and physical things. From day to day these elements grew stronger, her character more and more resembling our mother's.

Inwardly she was never free from fear, and that bothered him. "She has the most sensitive organism imaginable."

Her moods changed rapidly; she was constantly in danger, completely subject to her nervous system. She had been isolating herself from us more and more, withdrawing into herself. It had become a problem he didn't know how to solve.

To me it seems that she has already moved too far away from us for us ever to catch up with her again. Both of us lost our mother at the most devastating moment, but for my sister this loss may possibly have been fatal.

At first, my father said, he had placed my sister in a boarding school on Lake Constance. But that had been the worst thing he could have done. Under the rule of stern, unyielding nuns she had plunged even more into melancholy, and from then on her state of hopelessness had been continuous.

For the past year at home she had fallen into a listlessness that cast a pall on the rest of us.

I keep trying to approach her, in letters from Leoben, but in vain.

It is not improbable, my father said, that her psychic illness is more and more affecting her organic state. "I'm always frightened for her."

He had once taken her to Zeitschach, my father said, and stayed at an inn for two days. For the whole two days she did not speak to him. And yet it had been a lovely vacation spot, the countryside beautiful and the weather perfect. She had got up late and gone to bed early, as if distraught over the place and its surroundings. She had been unable to treat the stay there as a holiday, which he had meant it to be, but only as an ordeal.

Another time he had driven down to Laibach with her, and then on to Trieste and Fiume—all in all a six-day vacation, during which he had arranged with another doctor to take his place at home. But he had not been able to alter her mood. She was visibly growing more depressed all the time. In general he had observed that her spirits sank even more whenever she moved into the light.

Among cheerful people who take life easily she was wretched. Pleasant surroundings irritated her. A bright day plunged her into still deeper melancholia.

When visitors came to the house, she withdrew and stayed in her room until they were gone, my father said. The kind of amusements that are customary in the country simply baffled her. She had no girl-friends either. Sometimes she would go out of the house in the middle of the night and wander around the village.

Her sleeplessness reminds me of my mother's sleeplessness.

When she leaves for what is supposed to be a longish stay in the Tyrol, in Salzburg, in Slovenia, she returns next day.

In spite of all this, my father said, she is attached, with a fondness she herself does not always understand, to us, to her father and brother.

Everything is easier for me, my father said; for her everything is difficult. We have been living together for so long and don't know one another.

Each of us is completely isolated, although we are so close.

All of living is nothing but a fervid attempt to move closer together.

I thought I had never heard my father speak so emotionally about us.

He could already see me finishing my studies and launching on a career that would not disappoint him, he said.

At this point he noticed that Frau Ebenhöh had fallen asleep. He stood up and looked to see whether I was still there. He felt embarrassed that I had been listening to him.

We looked out into the garden and saw a woman, the neighbor, I thought, coming toward us through the grass in rubber boots. She took off the rubber boots at the door and entered. She had bought all sorts of provisions for Frau Ebenhöh, as well as a bottle of red wine, which she placed on the table. My father knew her, and she him. Frau Ebenhöh awoke. Did we know about the murder in Gradenberg? the neighbor asked. Grössl had not yet been apprehended. This was the fourth crime this year in these parts, she said, and reminded Frau Ebenhöh of the strangled potter, the throttled schoolmistress, both from Ligist, and Horch, the Afling furrier, who had been shot. Unpacking the bread and butter, she said: "It's the sultry weather."

My father admitted that he had been to see the innkeeper's wife that morning. She had died in Köflach, he said.

The neighbor straightened Frau Ebenhöh's bolster, turned her, tautened the sheet. The sick woman had fallen asleep again when we took our leave.

Walking back across the Stiwoll marketplace to our car, we talked about my forthcoming examinations, about the relationships among the students in Leoben, about their boredom and their general weariness with life. About the frequent suicides precisely among the most capable students. It was remarkable, my father said, that it should be the wealthy who incline to suicide; first they succumb to boredom, the worst disease anyone can fall prey to in this world.

The Mining Academy in Leoben is good, I said, famous, and unjustly deprecated by its own students. I imagine it's one of the three best in the world, I said. In Leoben things are so arranged that you have to concentrate entirely on your studies to keep from going crazy.

I said I was not isolated, it was only that every day I had to exert myself anew to win the solitude I needed in order to make progress. Sometimes I was even rude, offended people I liked. But if my mind started to balk at studying, I would leave the dormitory, usually alone, and go walking along the bank of the Mur, thinking only of my work until I had conquered my restlessness. Often, however, I merely went down to the Mur, that brown, sluggish, viscous river, for the purpose of complete distraction. I would climb the northern hills and let myself dream while contemplating the outward aspects of nature. Whenever I looked at it, I said, and from any perspective, the surface of the earth struck me as new and I was refreshed by it.

Often, I went on, studying the quality of the air and tramping for miles northeastward, in the direction of the Semmering, gave me the greatest pleasure. It was almost a sense of rapture and probably stemmed from the feeling of being altogether free.

Speculating on the local geology near the Mur, I said, would often calm my mind and give me back the clarity I had lost by strenuous studying. My mind would feel receptive again.

For a long time now I had been regarding myself as an organism I could discipline on command by my own will power, I told my father. To be sure, I sometimes had relapses, but these did not plunge me into despair. It was worth making the maximum effort to shake off a tendency to despair, I said. Better to be terribly strained than despairing.

There were moments when I felt empowered to see right

through the whole of creation. "Moments of pure *recrea-tion*," I said, though they left me exhausted.

Every day I completely built myself up, and completely destroyed myself.

Self-control, I said, is the satisfaction of using your brain to make the self into a mechanism that obeys your command.

Only through such control can man be happy and perceive his own nature. But very few people ever perceive their natures. To let the feelings predominate, to do nothing against the normal gloominess of the emotions, delivers people up to despair. Where the reason is in control, I said, despair is impossible. "Whenever this state of total irrationality closes down on me, there is nothing but despair inside me." Nowadays I only very rarely succumb to this state, I said. Life always seemed grim if you did not step outside it; the satisfaction came from enduring it rationally. Most people were governed by their emotions, not their reason, I said, and the result was that most sank into despair. "But the kind of reason I mean," I said, "is completely unscientific."

My father had been struck by my sudden loquacity. He commented that he too sometimes found himself talking about something, or even only seeing something he could not put into words, which was actually out of the question for people, was really humanly impossible.

Passing Bloch's house, we drove toward Hauenstein to call on a more or less crazy industrialist whose name I have forgotten. From Abraham we took a short cut over Geist-thal.

Students were always prey to a kind of restlessness, I said, because as long as they are at school they live in a no-man's land between the parents they have left behind and the world they cannot yet attain, and their instincts still draw them back to their parents rather than toward the world. There are often tragedies inside that no-man's land, which happen when they realize that they can neither return to their parents nor step out into the world. In the last six months in my dormitory alone three students have killed themselves, I said. Up to the last, there had not been the slightest symptom of emotional or psychic trouble in any of the three.

I myself had never even thought of taking my life, I said. But my father remarked that the idea of suicide had always been a familiar one to him. Even as a child, when other ideas became too much for him, he had often sought refuge in this idea. But whenever the idea did come into his head, it had always taken the form of an alternative that made life possible, hence something rather restful, never something in its own right. Both of us were thinking how dangerous it was to have my sister continually absorbed in thoughts of suicide, either brooding about it or actually attempting it. From the time she was little she had inclined toward self-destruction. What had first been a bit of dramatics, my father said, might later develop into a genuine emotion that could end in the real thing.

Beyond Abraham the hills were covered with large orchards. The farmers had set out their casks of cider in the sun. The houses are old. There is hardly a more isolated region than that between Geistthal and Hauenstein.

We had stayed much too long in Stiwoll, my father said. He had been expected all morning in Hauenstein, which was where the industrialist had his hunting lodge. He had

retired there to devote himself to a literary work over which
he agonized, even as it kept his mind off his inner agony.
The man was not yet fifty; my father had known him for
some two years. His half-sister shared his solitude with him;
she was, as I would shortly see, perfect for this role—ideal, as
the man himself put it. He had bought the hunting lodge
some fifteen years ago from Prince Saurau, whom we would
next visit at Hochgobernitz Castle. Even as long ago as that,
the industrialist had began conceiving this literary work on a
"purely philosophical subject" that he would never talk
about. If he talked about it, the industrialist repeatedly told
my father, if he even began talking about it, he would then
and there ruin the work, which had made such notable
progress. And he would no longer be able to start again from
the beginning. He was wont to say that he worked day and
night, writing and destroying what he had written, writing
again and again and destroying again and again, but approaching his goal. Aside from his work he permitted himself no diversion except the briefest talks with his half-sister
in the library or in the kitchen, and then only for the purpose
of settling questions of the meals. Twice a week his half-
sister would go to Geistthal to shop, mail letters, and fetch
their mail. They had enormous supplies in their hunting
lodge in case of what they called "the disaster," which supplies were never touched. The half-sister was his mother's
daughter, by a Chilean father; and as we slowly neared
Hauenstein, my father explained their relationship. They
lived together like man and wife. She would withdraw to
her room immediately after admitting my father to the lodge
and reporting his presence, and she would reappear only to
let my father out again.

The industrialist suffered from diabetes, my father said, and had to administer injections to himself every few hours. Twice or three times a month my father called to check on the state of his disease. As far as my father knew, the couple never received anyone else except himself. He had often asked people in the vicinity whether anyone ever visited the lodge, especially anyone from the city, but apparently no one ever did. The house certainly gave the impression of being inhabited solely by the industrialist and his half-sister. It felt as if no other soul had entered it for decades. It was not, as such hunting lodges usually are, filled with hunting gear, but was almost empty; it contained only the barest necessities. Even in the half-sister's room there was nothing but a bed, a table, a chest, and an easy chair. No pictures on the wall, not a picture in the whole house. The industrialist said he hated pictures. He wanted everything as empty as possible, as bare as possible. What little there was had to be as simple as possible. He regarded the dense woods around the lodge as a kind of wall. The mailman was allowed to enter this wall with telegrams, but not step inside the house; he had to call until the half-sister came to the door. There was a spring behind the house, my father said—excellent water.

We were now in a high valley and driving through nothing but woods and more woods.

There was not a single book in the industrialist's house, my father said; he deliberately kept books out of the house in order not to be irritated. After all, nothing is more irritating than books if you want to be alone, must be alone.

He allowed his half-sister to read newspapers, including *Le Soir, Aftonbladet, Le Monde,* and *La Prensa*—not a single German newspaper. But even these foreign papers had to be at least a month old so that, as the industrialist said, they would have no power of destruction, would be already poetic.

The industrialist's clothing was plain; my father had never seen him wearing anything but a shirt and slacks. He was said to speak not only all Central European languages, but also virtually all Far Eastern tongues.

Aside from a desk and chair, all he would have in his study was blank paper, so that he would be thrown entirely on his own resources and never diverted from his work. As for the subject-matter of his writing, he would say, he had the experience acquired in more than forty years in the metropolises of the world, in the industrial and commercial centers of all five continents.

His possessions were scattered throughout the whole world, chiefly in English-speaking countries. The industrialist ran his enterprises from Hauenstein; that took only an hour a day. A tremendously complicated apparatus, which was constantly in motion and included more than forty-thousand employees, was kept going from Hauenstein, and functioned better all the time.

When he was finished with his work—"which might possibly boil down to a single thought," he had once said to my father—he intended to leave Hauenstein again, depart from the mountains, turn his back on them.

The simplest kind of food sufficed him, he would say. Long walks, deeper and deeper into the woods, into the impenetrable "evergreen metaphysical mathematics," as he called the forests around Hauenstein, sufficed to keep his muscles from going slack. He was opposed to strolling and only walked in order not to "degenerate physically."

A small iron stove warmed his room, my father said; there was a similar stove in his half-sister's room. It was fortunate, he had once told my father, that he was diabetic, for that made it necessary for him to associate with one more person in Hauenstein beside his half-sister, namely my father. My father prevented "the perfect consistency of Hauenstein," he had once said.

It was apparent that the industrialist rarely talked, and that when he did he was trying to fend off something that was a cruel irritation to him.

The empty rooms always had a terribly depressing effect upon my father when he considered, he said, that the person who dwelt in them had to fill them solely with his own fantasies, with fantastic objects, in order not to go out of his mind.

The industrialist's sole occupation, aside from writing and walking in the forest and talking with his half-sister about the provisions, was shooting at a huge wooden target fastened to two trees behind the lodge. The desire to shoot overcame him from time to time, and of late more and more. "I'm practicing, but I don't know what for," he once said to my father. The gunshots could be heard throughout the vicinity, my father said; sometimes they went on for hours after midnight.

He alternated between total sleeplessness and total apathy for days at a time; there was no way for him to escape from this horrible state.

On normal days the industrialist rose at half past four in the morning and worked until half past one in the afternoon. Then he would eat a bite and work on until seven in the evening.

He allowed his half-sister the "greatest possible" freedom

in Hauenstein. But only six or seven weeks after they moved in he had spotted signs of insanity in her, "a madness rooted deep in clericalism." This insanity, the industrialist thought, might recede at once if his half-sister were to leave Hauenstein. In her extreme loneliness she was always close to the point of taking her own life. But her half-brother could see that out of sheer consideration for him, for whom she did everything though she did not understand him at all, she did not even permit herself a single loud outcry, or thrashing about, which might bring her some relief. My father, for his part, could see she had the withdrawn look characteristic of women in insane asylums. Incidentally, she was obsessive about cleanliness.

"Probably her half-brother has forbidden her to talk to me," my father said. "I always have the feeling that she would like to, but isn't allowed to."

He usually arrived in Hauenstein in the early morning, on the way to Prince Saurau in Hochgobernitz. "The air is purest then and the view of the Rossbach Alp at its most beautiful."

The road we were now driving on, he commented, had been built by the industrialist at his own expense. The whole length of it belonged to him. Everywhere, hidden in the woods, the industrialist had posted unemployed millers, miners, and retired woodsmen as guards whose task was to keep people from disturbing him.

My father said he thought the industrialist could spend a while longer in Hauenstein, a few more years, perhaps. As yet my father had not detected the slightest signs of madness in the man, unlike the half-sister. But no human being could continue to exist in such total isolation without doing severe damage to his intellect and psyche. It was a well-known phenomenon, my father said, that at a crisis in their lives some people seek out a dungeon, voluntarily enter it, and devote their lives—which they regard as philosophically oriented— to some scholarly task or to some imaginative scientific obsession. They always take with them into their dungeon some creature who is attached to them. In most cases they sooner or later destroy this creature who has entered the dungeon with them, and then themselves. The process always goes slowly at first. Yet my father was not inclined to regard the industrialist as an unhappy man. On the contrary, he was leading a life that suited him perfectly, in contrast to his half-sister, who on his account was compelled to lead a totally unhappy life.

At first such persons as the industrialist's half-sister try to defend themselves, my father said. They do not want to be wholly at the mercy of their oppressor. But they soon see that fighting back is useless. They cannot help themselves. Then they become attached to their oppressor with a despair that systematically destroys them. "The cruel despair of servitude," my father called it.

Because they are ruthless to the core, such people as the industrialist attain their goal, even though everyone else regards the goal as senseless and the method by which it is attained repulsive.

When we arrived at the hunting lodge, I saw that it indeed stood in a clearing and the whole picture conformed to what my father had said about it.

There was not a single trophy in evidence. The place did not look like a hunting lodge at all. I thought at once: a dungeon! A provisional dungeon! All the shutters were closed, as if the lodge were uninhabited.

The industrialist's study was at the rear, my father said. The man never allowed himself more than a single open shutter.

Everything in the place had to further the industrialist's concentration on his work.

We got out, and since my father was expected and our car must have been heard, the door was opened at once. The industrialist's half-sister led us quickly into the vestibule, and it struck me that originally the place could not have been a hunting lodge, for there would not have been a vestibule in such a lodge, not in our district. Probably the building had once served some function in the Saurau system of fortifications. There was not a single movable object in the vestibule, aside from a heavy cord that hung from the ceiling. The purpose of this cord perplexed me.

My father said I was his son. The industrialist's half-sister did not shake hands with me, however. She slipped away, leaving us alone in the vestibule. I was struck by how quickly she had bolted the front door again as soon as we had entered, thrusting a heavy wooden bar into a slot. Accustomed to my father's visits, she did not apologize before she disappeared.

I followed my father through several rooms that received some faint light through the leaves of the shutters. The walls were whitewashed, the floors larch planks. We had to go upstairs to the second floor. There was a long corridor, just as dark, determinedly darkened. I thought of the interior of a monastery.

We walked cautiously, but nevertheless made far too much noise because the rooms were empty.

I wished I could scream at the top of my voice, and as I

screamed wrench open the shutters. But reason checked me.

At the industrialist's door my father stopped, knocked, and entered without me when the industrialist called. I waited outside as we had agreed.

For a long time I heard nothing, then words (but could make out little of the context), finally a clear reference to the industrialist's literary work. He had made enormous progress during the past week, he said, and expected to go on making enormous progress. "Even though I have destroyed everything I have written up to now," he said, "I have still made enormous progress."

He was now prepared to go on working for years. Possibly the work would destroy him. Then: "No," he said, "I won't let myself be destroyed."

Then he spoke of his current business affairs, which were focused more and more on the African countries. He had received the most gratifying news from London and Cape-town, he said. Africa was developing at tremendous speed into the richest continent in the world, and it was essential to exploit the fact that the whites were withdrawing from it. "The white race is done for in Africa," he said, "but *I* am just beginning there!"

Coming back to his writing, he said that right now, "these past few weeks," he had made discoveries that were decisive for his work. His isolation, "the emptiness here," was enabling him "to reach out to a whole tremendous cosmos of ideas." Now everything was coming to fruition inside him. And he was mustering all his strength to complete his work.

In order to have nothing around that might interfere with his work, he said, he had ordered destroyed "the last real distraction I have had in Hauenstein." He had ordered all the game that still remained in his forests to be shot, collected, and distributed preferably to "the poorest people" in the whole vicinity.

"Now I no longer hear anything when I open the window," the industrialist said. "Nothing. A fabulous state of affairs."

After a prolonged silence in the room I heard my father speak of me to the industrialist, saying that I had come home for the weekend from Leoben, where as the industrialist knew I was studying at the Mining Academy, and he had taken me on his rounds this morning. I was outside in the corridor now. But the industrialist was not tempted to call me in. "No," he said, "I don't want to see your son. A new person, a new face, will ruin everything for me. Please understand, a new face would ruin everything for me."

The industrialist asked my father where he had been that day. It sounded like a routine question that he always asked.

"In Gradenberg," my father said. "An innkeeper's wife there was killed by a miner named Grössl. Then we were on the Hüllberg. And in Salla. And in Köflach. In Afling and Stiwoll."

"Are you going up to Saurau now?" the industrialist asked.

"Yes," my father said, "but before that I have to go down to the Fochler mill again."

"No," the industrialist repeated, "I prefer not to receive your son; I'd rather not meet him. When a new person suddenly turns up, it may be that he'll destroy everything for me. Just one person turns up and ruins everything." After a while the industrialist said: "Since all the rooms in this house are completely vacant, I cannot knock into any object in the darkness that fills them."

My father emerged. We went down to the vestibule. The industrialist's half-sister let us out. Even the clearing had something oppressive about it. "We'll drive to Geistthal for a bit," my father said. In silence we drove through the woods along the same road by which we had come, back to Geistthal. We did not see a soul. I was appalled, imagining that there was no longer any game in the forest and that invisible sentinels were watching us. Shortly before we reached Geistthal, we saw the first people. It was noon. At first we thought to drive to the Fochler mill by way of the Römaskogel, but then after all drove by way of Abraham to Afling, where we went to a restaurant that my father knew well.

All the tables were occupied. We were invited to come into the kitchen, where we were given preferential service. We heard talk about the killing in Gradenberg, and about the dead woman. Grössl had not been caught yet. But his hiding place couldn't be far away, someone said; sooner or later hunger would drive him into the open.

While we ate, my father again talked affectionately about the child in Hüllberg, then about Bloch. "They're all problems," he said. He opened his medical bag and saw that he had forgotten the books he had wanted to borrow from Bloch, the Diderot, the Nietzsche, and the Pascal. But anyway, he remarked, he would not have a chance to do any reading in the next few days. Frau Ebenhöh was taking much of his time. But the habit of visiting her would end soon, for she had only a few more days to live, would surely simply fall asleep. Then he began talking about the schoolteacher, the first person he had visited that morning, who had died under his hands. The fate of country schoolteachers was bitter, he said. So often they came from a town, no matter how small a one, where they felt easy, into a grim mountain community where everyone was hostile to them. Such transfers were usually made as a punishment. The teachers would lead a more and more wretched, depressed life, all the more hamstrung by the hateful regulations issued by the Ministry of Education. Most of them lapsed fairly soon into an apathy that might at any moment turn to madness. In any case they were people all too prone to regard life as a penance. But now, constantly in surroundings where they were not taken seriously, looked down on by everyone, their initially weak intellects were torn to shreds and they stumbled into sexual aberrations.

For the longest time, my father said, the sad fate of the Salla schoolteacher had preyed on his mind. But he did not want to talk about that case, he said. As soon as these words were out of his mouth, he apparently ceased to feel any need for secrecy, for he went on to say that in the Obdach grammar school there had been a scandal over the teacher's relations with a *nervous boy,* and the poor fellow had had to leave his post. He sought refuge in the Tyrol, then in Italy, and finally in Slovenia. For two full years, the man had lived like an outlaw, moving among people of foreign speech and subsisting mostly on small thefts. Then he had suddenly come back across the frontier, totally deranged, and had given himself up to justice. He was quickly brought to trial, and the court in Brock sentenced him to two years in jail and two additional years in a milder house of correction. He served his sentence in Garsten. Released (I thought of Frau Ebenhöh's brother), he had returned to his parents, who owned a small farm in Salla and who had nursed him lovingly. "Of course you could say that the teacher died of heart disease, of a so-called cardiac rupture—you could make it that simple," my father said. "But it wasn't that."

In the dying teacher's face my father had clearly seen, he said, a man's accusation against a world that refused to understand him.

The poor fellow had been twenty-six years old. His parents had had his shroud hanging up in the vestibule for weeks beforehand. "For weeks," my father said, "whenever I entered the house, the first thing I saw was his shroud."

The family had been relieved that he had died in the doctor's presence. They too, like Frau Ebenhöh in Stiwoll, must have regarded their son as a terrible punishment (from God?), my father said.

While we ate, my father also told me the following story about the deceased teacher. Once when he was a boy, his grandmother had taken him along into the deep woods to pick blackberries. They lost their way completely, wandered for hours, and could not find the way out of the woods. Darkness fell, and still they had not found the path. They kept going in the wrong direction all the time. Finally grandmother and grandson curled up in a hollow, and lying pressed close together, survived the night. They were lost all the next day and spent a second night in another refuge. Not until the afternoon of the second day did they suddenly emerge from the woods, only to find they had all along gone in a direction opposite from that of their home. Totally exhausted, they had struggled on to the nearest farmhouse.

This ordeal had quickly brought about the grandmother's death. And her grandson, not yet six, had had his entire future ruined by it, my father said.

You could always conclude that the disasters in a man's life derived from earlier, usually very early, injuries to his body and his psyche, my father averred. Modern medicine was aware of this, but still made far too little use of such knowledge.

"Even today most doctors do not look into causes," my father said. "They concern themselves only with the most elementary patterns of treatment. They're hypocrites who do nothing but prescribe medicines and close their eyes to the psyches of people who because of their helplessness and a disastrous tradition entrust themselves completely to their doctors. And most doctors are lazy and cowardly."

Putting yourself at their mercy meant putting yourself at the mercy of chance and total unfeelingness, trusting to a pseudo-science, my father said. "Most doctors nowadays are unskilled workers in medicine. And the greatest mystifiers. I never feel more insecure than when I'm among my colleagues. Nothing is more sinister than medicine."

In the last months of his life the teacher had developed an astonishing gift for pen drawing, my father said. The demonic elements that more and more came to light in his drawings shocked his parents. In delicate lines he drew a world "intent upon self-destruction" that terrified them: birds torn to pieces, human tongues ripped out by the roots, eight-fingered hands, smashed heads, extremities torn from bodies not shown, feet, hands, genitals, people suffocated as they walked, and so on. In those last months the bony structure of the young man's skull became more and more prominent. And he drew his own portrait frequently, hundreds, thousands of times. When the young teacher talked, the disastrous way his mind was set became apparent. My father had considered taking some of the drawings and showing them to a gallery owner he knew in Graz. "They would make a good exhibition," he said. "I don't know anyone who draws the way the teacher did." The teacher's surrealism was something completely original, for there was nothing surreal in his drawings; what they showed was reality itself. "The world is surrealistic through and through," my father said. "Nature is surrealistic, everything is surrealistic." But he felt that art one exhibited was destroyed by the very act of being exhibited, and so he dropped the idea of doing anything with the teacher's drawings. On the other hand, he was afraid the schoolmaster's parents would throw away the drawings or burn them—thousands of them!—from ignorance of how good they were and because they were still frightened, anxious, and wrought up about these drawings. So he had decided to take them. "I'll simply take them all with me," he said. He had no doubt they would be handed over to him.

The teacher's parents must have kept thinking of their sick son's unfortunate bent whenever they looked at him during his last illness, my father said. "What a terrible thing it is that when you know of some deviation, some unnaturalness, or some crime in connection with a person, as long as he lives you can never look at him without thinking about that deviation, unnaturalness, or crime."

From his bed the teacher had a view of the peak of the Bundscheck on one side and the rounded top of the Wölkerkogel on the other side. "You can feel this whole stark landscape in his drawings," my father said.

The teacher's parents said, however, that during his last

days he had not spoken at all, only looked at the landscape outside his window. But the landscape he saw was entirely different from theirs, my father said, and different from the landscape we see when we look at it. What he depicted was an entirely different landscape, "everything totally different."

We were not alone at our table for long. An elderly man, obviously the father of the restaurant owner, sat down with us. He kept asking us what we knew about the crime in Gradenberg. He did not let us eat in peace.

Down toward the Fochler mill the valley narrowed in a way that struck even him as sinister, my father said. I recalled that the mill is situated deep in a dark gorge; shortly beyond it the path winds up to the Saurau Castle.

We paid and left. In the restaurant a band of schoolchildren were being fed. They were given hot soup and admonishments not to make noise. What gruesome people these innocent creatures will inevitably become, I thought as we left the restaurant.

The Fochler mill is situated in the township of Rachau, but can be reached from Rachau itself only by a roundabout route forty miles long. That means that the mill is completely isolated. It lies directly below Saurau Castle, but the castle cannot be seen from the mill.

From Afling we drove directly into the gorge.

As it grew dark, I began thinking of my sister, whose wrist was still in a bandage.

A weekend was too short a time for me to be home from Leoben, my father said. We never got around to having a real talk. He himself, he said, could not have a good influence upon my sister, but possibly I could. Quite independently from one another, both of us had been thinking about my sister.

He used to watch her when she felt herself unobserved, my father said—when, for example, she stood musing in the garden, always at the same spot, staring fixedly at the wall of the shed. If he called her, she started and went to her room without a word. In his consulting room she was no help to him at all. She had the greatest dislike for everything medical. "In her I see my helplessness most plainly," he said.

His science had failed him worst of all in the case of his child, he often thought; the most it had ever given him were faulty predications. Sometimes he took my sister along to visit relatives, but she felt ill at ease in any kind of society.

I shifted his attention to a herd of sheep that briefly appeared on the ridge above the gorge.

As we drove deeper into the gorge, it seemed to me that hundreds and thousands of images were crowding into my memory, and I saw nothing more.

He had to visit the mill owner once a week to drain the pus from the man's ulcerated leg and change the dressing. It might amuse me, he said, while he was attending to this, to look at the aviary of exotic birds behind the mill. Now, as he mentioned the aviary, I remembered an association I had had with the Fochler mill. A funeral procession had passed by the Fochler mill on its way out of the gorge—I think it had probably come down from Saurau Castle—and the birds, hurling themselves in fright against the bars of the cage and disturbed by the intoned prayers of the people, had continually screeched at the funeral procession.

That had also been a Saturday. I reflected that most funerals are on Saturday. Baptisms, weddings, and funerals are almost always on Saturday.

But how different the mood was when we arrived at the mill this time. Two young workmen ("The sons," my father said) were loading a wagon with sacks of flour. The turbines were making so much noise that we could not hear ourselves speak. I could not understand what my father said to me before he entered the mill.

The shutters were of black iron. There were no flowers to be seen.

Above the front door the Saurau coat of arms could still be distinguished. This whole land must once have belonged to the Sauraus, I think. Castles like Hochgobernitz always owned mills and breweries.

My father had said that Hochgobernitz was situated on the height overlooking the gorge, but I could not see it.

The men carrying and loading the flour sacks had not noticed our arrival.

The river is so noisy here that you can hear nothing else in the whole gorge.

On the wagon stood a third young man, younger than the two others; he looked like one of the Turks, so many of whom are employed in our country nowadays, and in fact he was a Turk. He took the sacks from the shoulders of the miller's sons and piled them in regular order on the wagon. He was about my age, but not strong enough for the heavy mill work, which they do in the gorge today exactly as they did it centuries ago. But they produce their own electricity from the water of the river. Built adjacent to the mill, rising halfway above the surface of the water, is a power generator.

It occurred to me that the Turk had probably been in the gorge only for a few days. No doubt the miller's sons have spent most of their time making fun of him, I thought. I felt sorry for him. But at the moment Turks provide the cheapest labor in our country. That was the only sort they could have hired to work in this gorge. The Turks do the hardest work and put up with everything. He'll always have a rough time among these people, I thought; unless he promptly leaves, he's in for years of slavery. They did not give the impression of wanting to make the least thing easier for him. But you're only imagining that you are the Turk and ascribing your own thoughts to him, I reminded myself. Immediately, I also began relating the Turk to many people in whose field of tension he must exist—it's always my unfortunate way never to see just one person, the one I am looking at, but everyone with whom he may possibly be connected. Just as it's my way to look at each thing in conjunction with everything imaginable. I can't help myself. How destitute the Turk's life at home must have been for him to end up in this gorge in Central Europe, I thought. The gorge is a cruel betrayal of him.

But probably all this is quite different from the way I am conceiving it, I thought, and unnoticed by any of the three men working I walked around behind the mill, where I imagined the aviary would be.

The cage was even bigger than I remembered it. But it was completely uncared for and held not even half the number of birds I had seen that first time. Have so many of them died? I wondered. The few that were still in the cage, perhaps fifty or so, had fluttered in panic to the rear wall as soon as I appeared. They had no feed and were thirsty. The water bowl by the wall was empty. Everything inside the cage indicated that the person who had cared for the birds was no longer around. Two parrots were shrieking the same words in unison. I could not manage to make out what they were shrieking. I discovered a hose attached to the fountain in front of the birdcage and filled the bowl with water. The birds all rushed to drink. But everything about them was hostile; their plumage was constantly changing color from their nervousness. A madman must have been raising these birds and been destroyed by it, I thought. For a moment I had the impression that a person was standing behind me, and I turned around, but there was no one. I walked rapidly away from the aviary to the front of the mill where the three young men, though the Turk was more boy than man, were finished loading the sacks of flour. The Turk had just jumped down from the wagon; surprised by my presence, he halted for a moment at the wall of the house, looked searchingly at me, then ran like a flash into the mill.

I wanted to get away from the mill and walked along the river a bit, along the deafening stream of water that rushed ruthlessly out of the gorge and toward the mill. But then I told myself that my melancholy mood would only worsen if I walked any deeper into the gorge, and I turned back.

But didn't mills, of whatever kind, always send me into a pleasant, in fact a happy mood? I thought.

When I looked at the mill, I saw the funeral procession that had passed by here six or seven years before, one of the most pompous I had ever seen.

If I had to stay in this gorge I would suffocate in no time, I thought. And to think that anyone here could hit on the idea of raising exotic birds.

Now I felt the need to be with my father.

Approaching the mill, I mused that it was associated to this day with counterfeiters and murderers, though all that lay more than a century in the past. The most evil deeds could be conceived and carried out easily in a place of this sort, I thought; and all at once I felt how uncanny the two miller's sons were, as well as the young Turk. Why had these people brought this young Turk into the gorge? What crime were they nurturing?

After I had studied the Saurau coat of arms over the entrance, I quickly entered the vestibule. The voices I heard in the house promptly gave me my bearings. I paused at the right-hand stairway when one of the two miller's sons suddenly called me from behind. He asked me to come with him, and I went out again.

The gorge was now even darker than before, although its atmosphere is always as lowering as before a thunderstorm. These people live continually in this thunderstorm atmosphere, I thought, following the miller's younger son to an outbuilding. Too rapidly, I crossed a rotten plank over the river behind the miller's son, fearing at every step that I would lose my balance.

At first I saw nothing in the outbuilding. But then, when I had become adjusted to the darkness and the curious smell, a smell of flesh, I saw lying on a long board across a pair of sawhorses a heap of dead birds. They were from the aviary, I saw at once, the finest exotic birds. The beautiful colors nauseated me. These slaughtered birds were in fact the most beautiful specimens from the cage, and I turned around to the miller's son with a questioning look.

All three of them, he said, he himself, his brother, and the new young Turk who had been working in the mill only for a few days, had gone to the cage first thing in the morning, even before sunrise (But a sunrise in this gorge is impossible! I thought). They'd taken half of the birds, the finest first, and killed them with as little damage as possible to their precious plumage. How? They had wound the birds' necks rapidly around their index fingers several times and squeezed the heads. I counted forty-two birds all together. After they were through with the day's work, they were going to finish off the rest, the miller's son said. His uncle, he said, had started raising birds about twenty years ago and lived only for those birds. He had died three weeks ago, and the birds had begun raising a terrible racket. It was driving them half crazy. At first they thought that the birds' screeching over the death of their protector would let up after a while, or stop entirely, but they had been mistaken. It had only grown more and more unbearable. "You have to realize," he said, "that that sort of noise sounds a hundred times louder in this gorge." It was nothing you could get accustomed to, and you couldn't ask a person to endure it. So yesterday their father had told them they could finish off the birds to shut them up. They had done a lot of thinking about the mode of execution, and finally had hit on the idea of not chopping off their heads like chickens, but doing it so there would be no sign of outward damage. That way they wouldn't have to part with the birds, the miller's son said. They'd all grown used to those marvelous birds, even though they weren't completely daft about them the way their uncle had been. They intended to stuff the birds themselves and fill a whole room, their dead uncle's room, with them.

He'd had the idea of setting up a bird museum at the mill, the miller's son said. It hadn't been easy to get at the birds. When they started taking the first birds out and twisting their necks, the shrieking had increased, of course, but then it had gradually come to a stop. By the time they were done killing this batch, the rest had fallen totally silent.

Now I understood why the birds had been so frightened

when I approached the cage, for from the very first moment I had thought that the birds were reacting unnaturally.

Their faces were all scratched up from capturing the birds, the miller's son said. But now, with their experience, they would be able to process the remainder much faster and more easily that evening, and by tonight they would have perfect peace. . . . At first his father had thought of selling the birds alive to a collector, he said, but to find such a collector would have taken too much time and in the meanwhile they would probably have gone out of their minds. It was hard to get to a taxidermist, too; that was why they wanted to stuff the birds themselves in their leisure time. His uncle, the miller's son said, had had nothing in his head but those birds. He had left a vast number of notes about his birds; undoubtedly they'd be valuable for a bird specialist. ("We're all fond of making notes!" the miller's son said.) The miller's son picked up one of the handsome birds and held it high, so that we could see it well, and described its fine points. The young man apparently knew a good deal about exotic birds, I thought. Possibly all the inhabitants of the mill had concentrated on those birds. He was able to identify them all correctly. Some, he said, came from Asiatic countries, others from the Americas, and still others from Africa. Most of them, however, were Far Eastern island birds, with not a single one from Europe, he said. His uncle had often sat in the aviary for hours, but none of the birds had ever attacked him. They all had names like Kalahari, Malemba, Mitwaba, Ching-tou, Koejijang, Amoy, Druro, Drirari, Cochabamba, Carrizal, and so on. He said he knew the most remarkable facts about birds from the hundreds of ornithology books piled up in his uncle's room.

But I could stand it no longer in the outbuilding where

those dead birds lay on the board as on a bier. Above all the smell made it impossible for me to stay any longer, and I went out. I distracted the miller's son, and thus myself, from the dead birds by starting to talk about life in the gorge. Did he know Prince Saurau? I asked. Yes, of course. Sometimes the prince unexpectedly came down into the gorge and visited the mill. He would sit down and say "incredible things." He always came on foot. When there were parties in the castle, they could be heard down in the gorge, the laughter and music and the shouts of drunken people. But of late there had no longer been any parties at Hochgobernitz, the miller's son said. The prince was keeping more and more to himself. They had received the mill as a gift from a Saurau who died in the last century. One evening at the castle the prince had made a wager that he would give the mill away directly if he could not shoot a certain twelve-pointer next day in the gorge. He had not shot the twelve-pointer and had forthwith given the mill to the Fochlers, who had been working it for two hundred years. "When the Sauraus make a promise, they keep it," the miller's son said. I remembered that my father had said the prince was as crazy as he was rich. My father came out as I approached the front door again with the miller's son. The miller's son laughed. Seeing him laughing that way, I also saw him making pseudo-geometric movements with his hands, the movements of twisting birds' necks.

We now drove deep into the gorge. At its end, where it was darkest, my father said, we would leave the car and walk up to the castle. It was a rather dangerous path, hugging the left wall of the cliff, but he was used to it and I was young and athletic enough to walk it without fear. The prince expects my father every other Saturday. From the

castle you could look down over the whole beautiful countryside, my father said. There was no other point like it in all
of Styria for seeing the lay of the land. You could see all the
adjacent provinces of Austria from Hochgobernitz, and toward the southeast you could look as far as Hungary. There
was a good road leading up to the castle from the other side,
but to reach it we would have had to make a detour of more
than fifty miles by way of Planhütte.

As we approached the end of the gorge, we talked about
the Fochler mill. My father described the miller as a heavy-
set man of sixty who was simply rotting beneath the skin; he
lay on the old sofa all the time, could no longer walk; and
his wife, who to judge by the smell of her mouth was under-
going rapid degeneration of the lobes of her lungs, had water
on the legs. A fat old wolfhound ran back and forth between
the two, from her sofa to his and back again. Were it not that
fresh apples were kept heaped in all the rooms, the smell of
the two old people and the wolfhound would be unendurable. The miller's right leg was decaying faster than his left;
he would never stand again. "When a funeral procession
moves through the gorge," my father said, "it's uncanny." So
he too had once witnessed a funeral in the gorge. The miller's wife could stand on her legs only for a few moments at
a time. The two of them lay in their room almost all the time
and occupied themselves with their dog. The animal, because it never went out of the room, was absolutely dangerous in its derangement. One of the two, the wife or the
husband, had to hold it whenever my father entered their
room. Because of the screeching of the birds in the last few
weeks the dog had gone racing back and forth between the
two people "like mad."

By disposing of the birds the people at the mill hoped above all to calm the dog, and thus the calm themselves. The miller had told my father that he had ordered the birds killed off chiefly because of the dog's condition. Both of them, the miller and his wife, had alternately been holding the dog's leash day and night. Since they had been condemned to their room for months by their illnesses, they had gradually lost control over their sons. The elder, whom the miller described as prone to violence—he had often hit his mother and threatened to kill both of them—had once attacked his father with a hoe and severely injured him. The boy who had shown me the dead birds in the outbuilding was a weakling, completely at the mercy of his older brother. All the people in the Fochler mill were feeble-minded, not insane, my father said.

At present one of the miller's wife's sisters was running the household. She was in Knittelfeld today.

There were four cows in the barn, my father said. I wondered what the cows grazed on, since there was nothing but forest all around.

I said that the "weak son" had shown me the dead birds in the outbuilding. It was curious, I remarked, that we should have come to the mill on the very day the birds had been killed, or rather were being killed.

All the while we were there, I said, I had been reminded of the funeral I had seen on my former visit to the mill.

Even the Fochlers had heard about the killing of the woman in Gradenberg—the murder, they kept saying. But my father had deliberately refrained from saying that he had been involved in the case.

A notary from Köflach wanted to buy their mill, my father said. To make a summer resort (!) out of it. The miller and his wife had mentioned the matter, but they had no intention of selling.

That was good spring water they had at the Fochler mill, my father said. Then he added: "There is an oil painting in the old Fochlers' room." He would guess it to be between three hundred and fifty and four hundred years old. It was not a painting of saints, he said. On the contrary, it represented two naked men standing with their backs to each other but their heads "completely twisted, face to face." He had long admired the painting, he said, and had always associated a great variety of "rather gruesome" ideas with it. "If you take it down from the wall where it must have been hanging for hundreds of years and get it out of that horrible room and put it against a clean white wall, all its beauty would come out." The painting was absolutely ugly and at the same time absolutely beautiful, he explained. "It's beautiful because it's true," my father said.

In many Styrian houses, he went on, especially places steeped in darkness, as in that gorge, valuable works of art had been discovered and brought to light in the recent past. They were all gone by now. Gripped by a mania for antiques, city people had systematically robbed the whole country of its art treasures in recent years, and left behind a proletarian wasteland.

The gorge narrowed still more. First hemlock instead of pines stood along the river bank. There must be trout there, my father said. If we weren't in such a hurry—because before seeing Prince Saurau he also wanted to look in on the Krainer children who lived in one of the low-roofed servants' houses right below the castle—he would stop and look for trout in the river.

I was feeling horrified by the thought that there were people living in a place situated where that mill was. And what people! The dead birds had all exuded an alien odor of decay, I said. Some people, like those at the mill, I said, were forced to live their lives in the kind of cruel solitude that prevailed in the gorge. They had no choice; they were bound to their house, to their meager source of income, to a river like the one we were now following to its source. Others, I said, like the industrialist, of their own free will deliberately entered such solitude as he and his sister had at Hauenstein. But even as I said that, I thought that no one does anything of his own free will, that it is claptrap to say that men have free will. Suddenly the world seemed to me completely eerie; never before had I felt it to be so eerie as now, while we were still driving into the gorge. Soon we could hardly see anything, but my father had known the road for years. Where nature is purest and most untouched, as here in the gorge, it is at its eeriest.

Had my father noticed, I asked him, that the Turk gave the impression of being utterly terrified? They had put him into the dead uncle's room, but he had fled it in the middle of the night and gone to the sons' room, where he had lain alternately in the bed of the one and the other and begged them not to throw him out. They would let the Turk sleep in their beds for a few days, the younger son had said, until he stopped being afraid, until he grew used to the gorge. They couldn't keep the Turk's name in mind, I said, nor had I been able to, and so they simply called him Turk. All the miller's sons knew about him was that he had seven brothers and sisters at home, and parents to whom he wrote, because why otherwise would he have bought so much letter paper in Knittelfeld before he left with the older of the two sons, who had hired him away from a construction company there? They had not been able to make him understand their reason for killing all the birds. They did not understand him because they did not know a word of Turkish; he did not understand them because he spoke hardly any German. The Turk had been terrified of both of them, the miller's son had told me, when he saw them wringing the necks of the birds as they were taken out of the cage. He had leaned against the wall of the house absolutely motionless. Of course he might well have thought they were *crazy*. Because it hadn't entered their minds how brutal that was, they had laid the first corpses right in front of the birdcage, where the other birds could see them, and these first they had killed simply by squeezing their throats, which caused blood to spurt out. But then one of them thought to wind the birds' necks around the index finger and break the spine; and for that they went behind the cage. The bird swooned anyhow as soon as the neck was vigorously crooked around the finger the first time. You could hear the backbone breaking under the head. Again and again they had called on the Turk to help them finish off the birds just the way they were doing it; they told him to fetch some more birds out of the cage, but he would not. Then, apparently, the Turk had suddenly understood and all alone had killed ten or twelve birds by their method, much more skillfully than they. He had also brought empty flour sacks and covered the birds with them as they lay side by side on the board with their dangling heads.

I suddenly felt that the only way to escape the depression that matched the prevailing duskiness of the gorge was to begin to talk about Leoben. It seemed to me when I abruptly spoke of Leoben that I was speaking of the outside world. I forced myself to see myself alternately in the Mining Academy and in the dormitory. I concentrated on a precise vision of my dormitory room. Now I am seeing the dormitory room and it is not empty, I thought. Now I am seeing the dining room, and I am in the dining room. I see the municipal square of Leoben and I am in the municipal square of Leoben. I see the engineering professors and I am among them, although I am not among them but in the gorge. In reality I am in the gorge. But I am also in Leoben in reality. Everything is *in reality,* I thought.

"For a long time now," I said, "I have felt not merely exposed to my studies, but more and more committed to them. And for a long time now I have stopped regarding them as fantastic." It was no longer so hard for me to discipline myself as it was at the beginning, I said. During the whole of the first year I had been more or less a pitiable victim of the melancholia rife among all the students, a melancholia that poisoned everything for everyone, and as a result had been capable of only the most ridiculous, the tiniest, progress in my science. But now everything seemed easy and clear to me. "I have been able to fend off bad influences, to keep them away from my body and my brain," I said. "I know what is useful." But it had been a terrible process, I said, and I had been able to escape from the monotony of my own mental blindness only by the greatest ruthlessness toward myself. Youth is a dreadful condition, I thought. But it seemed to me foolish to say anything of the sort to my father. I had long been giving him a false picture. I saw no good purpose in telling him that there were still many things that oppressed me, that I was by no means free from problems. Or that my problems were also increasing with time.

He may believe I had no problems at all, I thought. I go on deliberately giving him a false picture. Just at this moment I was not at all sure why. "I have always taken pleasure in resolving my problems myself," I said. Had I said too much? My father was not even listening to me. Perhaps he was thinking only of the two Krainer children, or of Prince Saurau. I am strong enough now to resolve everything by myself, I thought. Often I am ashamed of feeling that I am stronger than others, though this feeling keeps recurring. But I did not speak of that.

The most striking thing about me is my incommunicativeness, which differs entirely from my sister's incommunicativeness. My silence is the opposite of my sister's. And my father's silence, his incommunicativeness, is again entirely different. What I know of him is always too little for me to be able to put together a picture of him as he really is, I thought.

For a moment I thought: You intended to spend today with your sister.

Aloud, I said: "The unforeseen is what is beautiful."

I still have tomorrow, I thought, with relief. Tomorrow, Sunday, I'll get up early and take a very long walk with my sister. And talk with her. In Leoben, I thought, I spend the whole week in my room, shut up within myself in my room, more and more hermetically isolated from the outside world as the year draws to its end, I don't even allow myself a breath of air any more! I offend many people by isolating myself that way. If once in a while I weaken and engage in a conversation because the others press me, I am always sorry. Is there any other way for me? I must go to bed before eleven, I think, and I rise at five. If I let myself deviate by even a hair's breadth from my schedule, I lose my equilibrium. As a scientist the only way is to pass through the endless, dark, and most of the time almost entirely airless corridor of your science in order to reach life.

We parked the car beside the waterfall and began climbing the dangerous footpath as quickly as possible. We had to watch every step; it was not advisable to look around. In silence we soon reached the outer walls of the castle. The climb had not strained my father at all. That surprised me. Before us we saw the one-story house in which the Krainer children live. Young Krainer, the son of upstanding parents who have served the Sauraus all their lives, is crippled. His sister led us straight into his room. He had heard us coming for some time, his sister said, and was restless. Their parents had gone into the castle early in the day. Young Krainer was just exactly my age, twenty-one, but looked twice as old. He had a black nightcap on his head and extended his hand to my father like a madman. Not to me. I sat down on a chair just inside the door. From there I watched what was going on in the room. Krainer's sister said there was a draft from the window. She closed it. He had come today for a "general examination," my father said.

I had the impression that up here an even more absolute silence reigned than down there in the gorge. It was no longer so dark as in the gorge, but everything here was also under the influence of darkness. The Krainer house, I had seen as we arrived, lay permanently in the shadow of the castle. The air on this height is keen; when you look down you are plainly looking into a pocket of sultriness.

My father and his sister undressed the cripple. It seemed to me that my father must be the only person whom the young Krainers see, aside from their parents, who work in the castle all day and are at home only at night.

As we emerged from the gorge and reached the peak, my father had proposed that while he was at the Krainers' I walk on the lower wall of the castle. But I wanted to see the cripple and his sister. I had the impression that my father wished to keep me away from them. And so I went along just because he was averse to taking me with him. (Later, when we were descending into the gorge again, he told me that both Krainer children reminded him too much of his own; they were the same age as we, as myself and my sister, although "there was no real parallel.")

Young Krainer had much too narrow a cranium. His eyes seemed to be starting out of his head. When his sister drew the blanket away from his body, I saw that he had one long and one short leg. For a while I could not decide whether his right leg was the longer one or his left. Finally I saw that the short leg was the left. If he stood up and started to walk, I thought, his motion would be like a huge insect.

They had difficulty persuading him to calm down. If anyone touched him, my father said, a quivering would seize his whole body, and at such times he was dangerous. He could hit out, bite, spit. He constantly made movements that complicated their efforts to prepare him for the examinations. Several times he struck out at his sister's face. But my father finally succeeded in holding his arms down against the sides of the bed and at the same time in listening with the stethoscope. A smell characteristic of those who lie in bed for years filled the room. Krainer's body was damp. He would slowly lose his speech entirely, my father later told me, as the result of progressive deterioration in his whole body. Even now you could understand only a fraction of what he said. He produced his words as if he were spitting them out. Most of it sounded as if spoken in an Oriental language. The rhythm in which he articulated was related to his physical malformation. What he spoke was just as crippled as the boy himself. Now and then he suddenly flung his long arms into the air, then let them drop again and laughed. His stomach was like an asthmatic sphere that his arms anxiously cradled for long moments. His head was relatively small; you saw that most plainly when he held it toward his protuberant belly in order to hear better the noises inside his stomach. He kept twitching his face almost continually in furious distortions. When he sat up, he seemed to be bobbing constantly. Maybe he imagines he is riding, I thought.

The bed linen was clean, probably because they expected my father, I thought. At times his bed had to be turned into a regular cage; a grating was placed over it for that purpose. But now, according to his sister, he was having a quieter period and did not need the grating. My father had always advised the Krainers never to remove the grating from his bed, but they did not follow his advice. He thought that the sick man might suddenly leave his bed and possibly kill them. But his sister had been unable to bear the sight of the grating after a while. It was now in the attic. She could not endure keeping her brother in a cage. If only they never had to bring that grating down from the attic again, she said. Her brother could no longer get up by himself, she thought, and if he did fall out of bed now and then it wasn't as bad as having to see her brother continually in a cage.

My father took hold of the patient's head and the sister held his arms down. Suddenly he wrenched his arms and head loose and tried to jump up. But he did not succeed. Abruptly, he laughed. Evidently it amused him to have my father examining his head, listening. My father tapped his forehead, drew down his eyelids, then pulled them up. He also checked young Krainer's knee reflex. He would take a urine sample with him, he said. When he pulled off the nightcap, I was horrified because there was not a hair on young Krainer's head. I noticed yellow spots on his temples, the same yellow spots, only smaller, that were on his chest. These yellow spots were scattered over his whole body. He had a tormenting fungus infection between his toes, his sister said, and for that reason he kept making rowing movements with his legs all night long. He no longer slept, she said. She herself sometimes closed her eyes from sheer exhaustion, but it was nothing like sleep. His trembling and dribbling had been going on for a year now. He relieved himself in bed. "Often he hears an army marching through the gorge," she said.

Everywhere in the room, wherever there was space, were musical instruments on which young Krainer had been able to play when he was still healthy. There was a cello, and I saw an oboe lying on the chest of drawers. For years a music teacher from Knittelfeld had come up here to them and given him lessons. Her brother had learned the most difficult violin compositions by heart, she said. His favorite instrument was the cello, and Béla Bartók his favorite composer. There were hundreds of scores piled in the drawers of the chest, and he had learned them all by heart. He had done compositions of his own, including a *Magnificat*. As a child of eight he had already been able to play Mozart's symphonies on the piano by heart. Only six months ago she had brought the cello to his bed twice, once in the morning and once in the afternoon, and he had played it until he was exhausted.

There was an open sore on his back, I saw, and on his chest he had red as well as yellow spots.

The music teacher from Knittelfeld had come up from the valley for years "gratis," the Krainer girl said. "Often they played together half the night." But once her brother had for no apparent reason hit the music teacher on the head with his violin bow, and from then on they no longer saw the music teacher. Her brother's illness had immediately begun rapidly worsening.

On the drive home my father told me that young Krainer had been in the Steinhof asylum for four years. Throughout that time his sister had rented a tiny room in Ottakring in order to be near him. At first it had looked as if he would never get out of the mental hospital; the doctors always used the word "hopeless" when they spoke of him. But suddenly, after four years at Steinhof, after he had spent four years in the largest and most terrible of all European insane asylums, the doctors had suddenly told the girl she could take her brother home.

"At your own risk," they had said, while simultaneously declaring that he was not dangerous. For a while she had kept him in her room in Ottakring and shown him the capital. Whenever they walked in Vienna, they had created a great stir, for his deformity in conjunction with his madness had struck people as funny. But by then the Krainer girl no longer minded when people gawked at her brother. She showed him the Prater and took him to the opera and the Burgtheater. They also went to the Rebernigg circus. For a whole week they went about the city, visited St. Stephan's Cathedral several times, went to the Naschmarkt, even attended a concert by the famous cellist Casals, who was playing the Beethoven sonatas. But soon their dragging around the city tired him; after a week it bored him; and she regretted spending the money Prince Saurau had given her (the Prince had also paid for the stay in Steinhof) on seeing a city that by now only aroused disgust in her. They gave up the room in Ottakring and went back to Hochgobernitz. At first he had enjoyed taking long walks. He enjoyed the country-side. Nature meant a great deal to him. The two of them loved to walk to the cliff and look down into the gorge. Standing there, his sister explained to him the villages in the valley. During that period he had been more receptive than ever before. Soon he resumed playing the cello, the violin, and the piano. She took longer and longer walks with him. But once, when she had walked with him as far as the oaks, from where you can look directly down upon the Frochlers' mill, he had suddenly come up behind her and struck her on the head with a branch. When she came to, her brother was sitting beside her, weeping. They went home. That night, when she was sure he was asleep, she brought the grating from the attic and placed it over his bed. From then on she had the feeling that her brother hated her. But she loved him.

She seldom had a chance nowadays to go out of the house alone, to walk a bit toward the castle, into the castle yard, or on the castle walls. Whenever she did go out, she would always have to recount her adventures as soon as she got home. But it was a long time since she had seen or experienced anything, she said. "Yet if I don't tell him things, he threatens me," she said. Now and then he insisted that she powder his face to hide the redness of his constant fever.

The examination had been difficult but had taken only half an hour.

My father had actually made this totally insane and crippled young Krainer put out his tongue at the end of the examination. While he was filling out a prescription, I made a curious discovery: On the four walls of the room, which horribly enough had to serve as the bedroom for *both* the children because the house was so small, hung a number of large engravings—probably the property of Prince Saurau, I thought—representing the great men of music. At first I had not realized that all these engravings were of composers. But then I noticed that young Krainer had written on all of them in red ink. Above the head of Mozart he had written: "Very great!" and above Beethoven's head: "More tragic than I!" and above Haydn's head: "Swine," and above Gluck's: "Don't like you." Across Hector Berlioz's face he had written: "Horrible," and for Franz Schubert: "Womanish!" I could not see the two engravings above his bed so clearly, nor decipher their inscriptions. Young Krainer had been watching my efforts to decipher the inscriptions all the while, and when he saw that I could not make out those on the two engravings above his bed, he laughed at me. On Anton Bruckner's face was a contemptuous "Music-hall stuff"; on Purcell's, "Stop it, Scotty!" Beneath a large photograph of Béla Bartók he had written: "I am listening!" In the corner where I had been sitting all the while, I discovered before we went out three violins with their necks broken; the broken necks were bunched together with a cord. Young Krainer's restiveness had given way, now that the examination was over, to exhaustion. He let his sister lay his head back on the pillow without protest. He asked for water, and his sister brought him some in a tin cup. Probably, I thought, he often hurled drinking vessels against the wall after he had drunk.

Such deformity is always joined by the corresponding insanity, my father said when we were outside. "The physical disease leads directly to the mental disease."

I asked my father if he had read the inscriptions on the engravings. He said he had. Young Krainer had once carefully explained to him what all these legends meant. Incidentally, he wrote over or smeared over every piece of paper that came into his hands, my father said; he had scribbled thousands of curious remarks on the scores in the chests. "A person like young Krainer can live on to be terribly old," my father said. He was taking me with him for the sake of my studies, my father said. He repeated that again and again: "For the sake of your studies."

# THE PRINCE

I T actually was a view for hundreds of miles in every direction.

Up to now I had only heard of Hochgobernitz—the castle. Now I was seeing it in reality.

Because we were expected, the gate was opened at once for us, and we were told that the prince was either on the outer or the inner wall. We saw him on the outer one.

On the way there my father explained that aside from the prince only his two sisters and two of his daughters were living in the castle. The prince's only son was studying in England. Finally we came upon Prince Saurau on the *inner* castle wall, walking and talking to himself.

He greeted my father and me casually. He had been having all sorts of curious thoughts about the events of the morning, he said. When he greeted us, he had not paused in his walk; we joined him. Our presence seemed not to disturb him. From here, I thought, you probably had the finest view of the entire country.

Prince Saurau said that he had evidently overestimated the difficulty of finding a new steward after the old one's death. Just this morning, the very day his advertisement had appeared in the newspaper, three men had already presented themselves: a man of thirty-four, named Henzig, who at first

seemed to him too young; another of fifty, named Huber,
who seemed to him too old, and a man of forty-two, named
Zehetmayer, who knew nothing at all about forest manage-
ment, a poor madman, who came originally from farm stock
in the Puschach Valley and was a former schoolteacher.
Zehetmayer had appeared shortly after eight o'clock to apply
for the post of steward at Hochgobernitz. He was a man
equipped with numerous talents, but all of them ultimately
disastrous for him. And considering his age of forty-two he
was in a shameful physical state (heart, lungs, and so on).
The prince had quickly made it clear that this post of steward would be far beyond his strength, and that it would be
helpful neither to the prince nor himself if he hired him.
"Not even on probation," the prince had said. "No, I won't
hire you even on probation!" The two others had turned up
immediately afterward, Henzig at ten, Huber at eleven. "I
dealt with them in the office," the prince said. "There was no
need of my convincing Zehetmayer that it was pointless for
him to enter my service, that this post as steward entailed the
very highest demands and the most difficult conditions. But
in general, I said—and it was ridiculous to have to say it—in
general, I said, I had the impression that the man was over-
estimating his strength. You overestimate your strength by
far! I said, and Zehetmayer, naturally enough, because he
isn't stupid, Zehetmayer did not say a word in protest to
what I said to him, and I said nothing but remonstrances. Of
course, every objection I had to make against him," the
prince said, "had the greatest impact. Indeed I felt that at
once: This is a man I can speak to with complete honesty.
Although he is weak, although his whole constitution is
weak, the weakest imaginable, I need not handle him with

kid gloves; I can tell him straight out everything I think, and I thought (at first) nothing good about the man, for I instantly saw through him, yes in the very moment he entered the room, like a tragedy that suddenly steps straight into my room. It was as if I saw a life-size and then a more than life-size stereotype of a primordial human tragedy whose name is Zehetmayer, Augustine Zehetmayer." The prince said: "This whole man in his comfortable but cheap clothes is nothing but the stereotyped image of all human poverty and inadequacy. What *I* said and what *he* said, everything *I* did and everything *I* thought and what *he* did, pretended to do, what *I* pretended to do and what *he* thought, it was all this stereotype, this stereotyped idea of the inadequacy, poverty, frailty, inferiority, deathly weariness of human existence, and I instantly had the impression that a sick man had entered my house, that I was dealing with a sick man, with someone in need of help. Whatever I said was spoken to a sick man, Doctor, and what I heard, Doctor, came from the lips of a sick man, from an extremely submissive, morbid brain which is filled with the most fantastic but embarrassingly derailed notions that in themselves reveal him for what he is. . . . The man had no idea of what he wanted, and I made him aware of this in the most forceful way; I said that what he was doing was morbid, that his whole life was a morbid life, his existence a morbid existence, and consequently everything he was doing was irrational, if not utterly senseless. Irrational for him to apply for the position as steward. A kind of mysterious megalomania was clearly expressed by that act on the one hand, since he lacked all the prerequisites for the post, did not have the slightest qualification for it, I said. But I could well imagine what had prompted him to follow up my advertisement. Irrational, I said," the prince said. "A person reads a newspaper notice offering a position which this person knows he will never obtain because, as I said, he completely lacks the prerequisites for this position, but the notice haunts him, he can no longer tear himself away from it, he simply can't escape it, he applies for the post, he knows it is absurd to apply for the post, he recognizes that everything he does in connection with the newspaper notice is absurd, everything, and yet he follows it up. I can well imagine, I said to Zehetmayer," the prince said, "that a person reads a notice and thinks that this notice has been inserted for no one but himself (certainly!) and that the person is completely captivated by the notice and applies for the opening, no matter how irrational that may be. Since he, Zehetmayer, was fully aware that he had not the slightest prerequisite for the steward's position I advertised, since he is aware, has always been aware, that he is a schoolteacher and knows nothing about forestry in practice let alone as a science, that he doesn't understand nature because he believes in the simplicity of nature as a helpless victim of nature, because he is always inside nature, therefore it is nothing but morbidity to apply for the steward's position. It was, as I said to Zehetmayer," the prince said, "a piece of trickery, more so of himself than of me, for that I am being tricked when he applies for the advertised position of steward was quite clear. . . . I did not say," the prince said, "that everything within which and by which Zehetmayer exists and has always existed up to now is deception, even though that is true, but I did say that a deceptive element has already been his downfall. I imagine the most disastrous family situations in connection with him," the prince said. "I tell Zehetmayer: I suppose you had an overwrought, abnormal childhood. But the man doesn't understand me. I think he comes from the Puschach Valley where they speak that awful dialect and doesn't understand me, and then I realize at once as I speak the sentence 'I suppose you had . . .' and so on," the prince said, "that the man doesn't understand me and not only because he comes from the Puschach Valley. I realize that when you're talking to such a man (and to such *people,* of course!) you have to speak simply, you must not voice anything complex, anything that strains the mind. With such a man as Zehetmayer you must not commit the crime of your own nature, I mean the crime of thrusting him into your own thoughts, into your vast and endless labyrinth of numbers and figures and ciphers, the maze of your own nature. The greatest crimes," the prince said, "are committed in words by superiors against inferiors, I think, crimes committed in thoughts *and* in words. In his first few sentences vis-à-vis me Zehetmayer began to perceive that his presence in my house [The prince did not say: in my *castle*] is nonsense. Sitting opposite me, with mechanical apathy he keeps moving his immobility the whole while. Whenever he opened his mouth to say something that he after all did not say, didn't dare to say, I was able to study what was grotesque about him. I studied the grotesqueness of his very presence, not only in connection with him and with him as a human being, but also in connection with me, in connection with everything between him and me, me and him—in connection with everything. He said he had read my notice at breakfast and all at once innumerable images all related to my notice had come to him; images that all had their source in my notice, had been projected from it into his brain. He said that in different words," the prince said, "but in any case it was a projection. Zehetmayer did *not* say: A film suddenly flashed through my brain, its sequences all related to the newspaper notice, translated into excitement. Instead, he said, in keeping with his nature: I could *think* of nothing else but that notice in the newspaper. And he said: My wife discouraged me from coming here; she wants me to apply for a position but she thought this one a bad idea. She said he wasn't fitted for this post, that he was a teacher. She said to him: You're a teacher; and she said, as she invariably did: A bad teacher. Zehetmayer said: I dressed and came here. After Zehetmayer said the words *came here,*" the prince said, "after Zehetmayer had spoken the words and left them hanging in the air, I repeated them, I had to take them out of the air, bring them down to earth again, clear the atmosphere for what followed. Zehetmayer said," the prince said, "that at this moment it was a mystery to him why he was applying for the position. But we do so many things which remain a mystery, he said. You see, my dear Doctor, he said: I don't know why. He reads the newspaper every day and he always reads all the ads; Zehetmayer reads them under pressure from his wife. His wife works and earns money. He finds reading employment ads a bore and he had never before reacted to any of them as he reacted to my notice. I wondered," the prince said, "whether my notice might not have been written in a remarkable way. But I didn't think so. (Steward for large forestry enterprise wanted . . . Saurau . . . and so on. . . .) My ad is composed in a wholly uninteresting tone. There's nothing stimulating or enticing about it or in it. I wrote it quickly and sent it to the newspaper, and I was surprised myself at how impersonally, how unattractively, it is written, although originally, of course, I'd intended to compose an individualized, attractive advertisement, or at least an interesting one, not an uninteresting one. . . . I sent it in and thought: Your advertisement is pointless, not a soul will respond to it. And so on. . . . And then," the prince said, "Zehetmayer called on me early this morning, and right after him these two other applicants appeared, Henzig and Huber, and I think still more applicants will be coming up here to see me, for it is hardly likely that these will be the first and the last. After all, I think, my advertisement must be fascinating, to judge by the effect. I have a very definite notion of a fascinating ad, I think, but suppose this one happens to be particularly fascinating just because it's not fascinating. . . . To think that things have come to such a pass, Doctor, that a Saurau has to insert an advertisement," the prince said. And then: "I said: Herr Zehetmayer, can it be that you sincerely think that you know anything about forestry? To that he replied: No, I don't know anything about it, really, I don't know the slightest thing about it, for the fact that I grew up in the country, he said, doesn't mean that I know anything about forestry. Naturally not. I poured him a glass of whisky (I myself haven't drunk anything for weeks, Doctor, since you've told me I mustn't) and asked the man, for the question seemed perfectly natural, why he was no longer a teacher. It was after all unusual, I said, no longer to be a teacher at forty-two for a man who *is* a teacher. My thoughts, Doctor, the language itself, Doctor, have suddenly become all strange to me again! He said that he had been discharged from the educational system ten years ago. His pension rights canceled, he said. He said he had been accused of a crime (rape?) that he hadn't committed and for which he had spent two years in prison and three years in the Garsten Reformatory. It was impossible for him to tell me the nature of the crime, he said. (Rape?) He said he had enjoyed teaching, had above all appreciated the freedom that the profession of teaching permitted, the *daily cleanliness* in which a teacher was able to move, his lovely world of possibilities in the country. (Yes, to be a teacher! he exclaimed.) No," the prince said, "he lived on his wife's earnings, granted, on her strength, and was basically without hope. So this morning he had read the notice and followed it up. *Zehetmayer,* he said, and actually, Doctor, he said it ironically, which astonished me. I could look it up, he said, the name of Zehetmayer was that of an old Styrian family of cattle dealers and weavers, come down in the world." The prince laughed. "The name doesn't amount to anything any more, Zehetmayer said. Suddenly," the prince said, "Zehetmayer was explaining everything. One of these mountain intellectuals gone to seed, I thought. Undoubtedly, I thought, crazy. A man who has simply let himself fall into the easygoing apathy of his begetters, simply because it is too great an effort to save himself. It's foolish, Zehetmayer said, but as I read the notice. . . . He took pleasure in the sentence he had begun but abandoned, tossed away unfinished," the prince said. *"Yes,* no desire, *no,* no desire, no desire, Zehetmayer said. He stood up as if he felt himself in that accursed relation with nature for a moment even more ridiculous than he had so far been able to be. By the way he stood up," the prince said, "and went out of my office, he emphasized this ridiculousness. Does he enjoy misery? I thought. Foolish, Zehetmayer said once more and went away, with an absolute mania for self-torment. I thought, here a man turns up who says his name is

Zehetmayer, and the man's no use to me at all. Pointless," the prince said. "Immediately I observed several already advanced diseases in the man, probably venereal diseases as well, such as are typical of this region. The people of northeastern Styria have one unmistakable characteristic, an infinite tendency toward inbred mysticism, a special clotted rhythm of language and movement. I say the words Puschach *Valley* and the man is ready to tell me a long story about an experience of his on Puschach *Lake*," the prince said. "In general I am struck by how readily people react to specific words, to sentimental words to which they immediately attach a sad tale that they once experienced and that once made a deep impression on them. Now Zehetmayer," the prince said, "once fell out of a boat on Puschach Lake. You know Puschach Lake, don't you, Doctor?" My father said, "Yes." The prince said: "His elder brother tried to pull him up over the side of the boat, but couldn't manage it. Zehetmayer spent five hours in the water until his father came along in another boat and pulled him out. The site of the accident is six hundred feet deep, but even if it had only been twenty-five or thirty feet deep, and so on. . . . Zehetmayer said he couldn't have stayed above water by his own strength another five minutes. He's a type who is extraordinarily susceptible to certain conceptual words that are all more or less connected with frightful personal experiences. The two words *beautiful view,* which I said remembering a beautiful view, instantly led him to another though shorter story, but one no less unfortunate than the one about Puschach Lake. He related, or rather sketched," the prince said, "how in the vicinity of the Bellevue Inn in Salla he was attacked by an escaped convict, and that only two weeks after

he himself had been released from the Garsten Reformatory.
. . . The man attacked Zehetmayer from behind and stole
his wallet. He had had only twenty schillings in the wallet,
but unfortunately it also contained the one photograph he
possessed of his mother. The robber was caught, tried in
Linz, and sentenced to twelve years in jail. Probably, according to Zehetmayer," the prince said, "he's out again by now,
after serving four years. I know what justice is like in this
country, Zehetmayer said," the prince said. "Actually I
should have taken care not to use exciting words in his presence, and not only in his, incidentally. Zehetmayer is another
of those innumerable persons who react to certain words, possibly those that have some permanently horrible association
for them, in an absolutely shattering manner. With my father, for example," the prince said, "I always had to avoid the
word *aslant,* and the words *sausage, Auschwitz, S.S., Cri-
mean wine, Realpolitik.* For everyone there are certain words
that must be avoided. My sisters, my daughters, my son, all
suffer from this kind of reaction; there are certain words
which cause them hopeless torment. It occurred to me that to
Zehetmayer I probably must not mention the word *mole.*
But suddenly I found myself saying, probably in order to test
him, *That's a terrible place for moles, the Puschach area.*
And I observed that his whole person was instantly plunged
into a state of torment. I had actually had the feeling right
from the start that I must not confront Zehetmayer with the
word mole. (With his native place!) I confronted him with
it, and my assumption that it pained him when I said the
word *mole* (reminding him of his native place) was con-
firmed. I also must not, it became clear to me, say such words
to him as *puke, Bundscheck, linen, miners,* nor *mine,* nor

the word *reformatory*. But I must admit," the prince said, "that all the time Zehetmayer was there I felt constantly tempted to use precisely these words he found so dreadful. For instance," the prince reminded himself, "you kept saying the word *turnips*. I did not spare him," the prince said, "I certainly did not spare him, not for a moment. Zehetmayer is the type of person who should be spared, just as most people should be spared, Doctor, but I did not spare him, right from the start I saw all his weaknesses and ailments and for that very reason I used no consideration toward him. I do not have to be considerate of this man, I told myself for just one moment, the crucial moment. It won't do him any good, no good at all, and so on. . . . Why? My dear Doctor, I keep falling into such utterly foolish questions," the prince said, "questions that aim at an explanation, at illumination. But there is nothing to explain, nothing to illuminate. At the name *Stainz*," the prince said, "the name *Rassach* came to Zehetmayer's mind (not mine!), and in connection with Rassach another story. You will have to hear this story," the prince said. "Zehetmayer's existence apparently depends solely on the stories connected with those special words, which stories he is obliged to tell whenever such a word is mentioned. In Rassach," the prince said, "Zehetmayer has relatives, and one day as a child he was playing in their hayloft. It was afternoon, Doctor, and in that airless hayloft there was that stifling heat which children think might kill them with no parents around to save them. You know that terrible hayloft heat. Suddenly Zehetmayer, then four years old, was called to supper by his uncle. He started and turned around, and started once more, for he saw a man's body hanging from a beam. *A hanged man,* Zehetmayer says. He

called out to the hanged man, told him to jump down from
the beam, because at four he imagined that the man could
jump easily from the beam. *Supper time,* the child kept saying, *supper time,* again and again. The dead man was the
first totally naked person Zehetmayer had ever seen. Suddenly the four-year-old became aware that the man hanging
from the beam was *dead,* and he let out a scream that
brought the whole family rushing into the hayloft. Someone
they did not know had hanged himself from the beam,
probably the night before, according to Zehetmayer. *In a
state of agitation.* (Zehetmayer today.) Zehetmayer then described how his uncle, in order not to have to cut the rope,
worried the head of the corpse out of the noose, how the
family puzzled over who the suicide might be. They
searched the pockets of his clothing, which was lying on the
floor (nothing but shirt and jacket), but found nothing.
Again and again," the prince said, "they looked alternately
at the corpse and at the boy who had discovered it, little
Zehetmayer. Then the uncle suddenly said: *The poor kid!*
And at that Zehetmayer, terrified, ran off, ran from the hayloft into the house and out of the house into the woods where
he lost his way, cried . . . and so on. While Zehetmayer was
telling this story which was bound up with the name *Rassach* (*Stainz,* and so on) I realized that the man was not entirely sober. The whole time it had not occurred to me that
Zehetmayer might be drunk. I thought: Possibly he was
drunk at the time he left the house, and then I thought:
Zehetmayer is drunk continually. There are quite a number
of other oddities to tell in connection with this man Zehetmayer," the prince said. "But I'll forbear. I watched him as I
have never yet watched anyone else leaving the place, until

he was outside the walls. Until he simply disappeared from sight.

"Nine o'clock," the prince said. "I read through my advertisement once more and reflect that it is a perfectly ordinary, not especially attractive notice. It surprises me that there should be a single person who comes in response to it, and then the two other applicants arrive, Henzig and Huber. First Henzig," the prince said. "Let me give you a brief sketch of Henzig." (Something hysterical about the prince's tone!) "Thirty-four years old," the prince said. "Henzig seems to me excellently fitted for the post, though I didn't like him (in contrast to Huber, whom I found more likable than naturally fitted for the post). Henzig comes from the vicinity of Aussee, son of a family of foresters. His father is a commissioner of forests; he attended the School of Forestry, studied soils, and so on. . . . Sureness about everything he says; moreover, everything he says is *correct,*" the prince said. "Strip selection cutting—opening up the canopy—shelterwood, etc. I was stunned by the way the man knew everything. (Vertical group selection cutting, etc.) But I felt dislike for the man's neatness," the prince said. "Personal cleanliness, clothing, and so on—all merits that suddenly repel me. Why? I don't have to look at the references to know that I'm dealing with an excellent man. Right at the beginning of the interview with Henzig I had to laugh the name Zehetmayer away. A poor wretched fellow, I say to myself, and let Henzig give me a summary of his previous employment while still savoring the unspoken name *Puschach Lake.* I had my mind on Zehetmayer, not on Henzig, Doctor. I had my mind on Zehetmayer's generalized despair while Henzig was giving me specific data on his career. Suddenly I said

aloud: Of course there are people who are so horribly constituted that they occupy one's mind continually, and in a
*pleasant* way, moreover. Henzig was irritated," the prince
said, "but only for the briefest moment. Then he went on
with his summary. It was a pleasure for me to listen to Henzig and to think of Zehetmayer," the prince said. "I had no
difficulty in carrying this amusement to an extreme. Henzig
said that he had been working for six years in Kobernausserwald, *certainly the foremost forestry school in Austria,* in the
former Habsburg, now republican, state forests. Henzig said
something about Douglas firs, about arid and humid strata,
*broad base,* about conditions of payment, purchases and
sales. I heard the name *Liberia* and the word *mangroves;*
and several times, sounding very grotesque: *The Habsburgs.*
It would have been wise to hire the man on the spot," the
prince said. "For I realized at once: Here is a top-notch man.
But I did not hire him then and there," the prince said. "This
man reminded me of my youth, of long walks in the woods
with Forest Commissioner Siegmund. Of conversations
about the colors of game birds, fees for hunting licenses, tree
diseases, sale of lumber to France and Italy, of my young
manhood. I suddenly found myself looking through him
into long and in any case secret and faded talks. The smell of
all these talks and subjects and woods and clothes were in
my nose, and the smell of the air on the banks of the Ache,
the smell of Tyrol, Salzburg, Upper Bavaria, and Upper Austria, the smell of kindred forests. I looked into an official
building on the margin of a Tyrolian forest, where the floor-
boards betray who is walking on them. You hear such
phrases as: *The forest commissioner is coming!* or *Dr.
Konstanz* or *Marie* is coming. The door opens into a library

in which two thousand volumes of distorted history are lined up, from Descartes and Pascal to Schopenhauer and the obscure Schlern papers. When I looked through Henzig I saw the vast forests between the inn and the lowlands of Bavaria, or the endless woods of Slovenia," the prince said. "I kept thinking: The tranquility of nature is and remains an infinite tranquility. Suddenly I said to Henzig: All in all," the prince said, "and I said that in extreme embarrassment, all in all you seem to me too voung for the post. For you must realize, I say to Henzig, that you would be bearing an enormous responsibility entirely alone. In the Kobernausserwald, I say, there are many state employees, and no matter how good they are, they bear no responsibility. State employees do not bear responsibility. Under the Republic the word responsibility has become a foreign word! I say. I know it, I say to him," the prince said, "in the state forests everything is irresponsible; that is the most conspicuous characteristic of these so-called new, but actually age-old systems: that there is no responsibility in them. And I say," the prince said, "you see the consequences of this irresponsibility of course, my dear fellow. Of course you see them, I said, I mean, I said, I know what I mean by responsibility. In this position you have the utmost responsibility. In this post there is no such thing as this ridiculous Republic. On the Saurau property this ridiculous Republic doesn't exist. Not yet, I say. This is a state in itself. Here, I say, our own laws prevail, the Saurau natural laws. Understand, I say, the Saurau laws of nature, not those of the Republic, not those of the pseudo-democracy. And I say: The area is vast; you surely know how large the area of the Saurau property is, *still* is. Henzig says he does. Well then, I say, and you mean to say you feel equal to such a position? Let me call your attention to the fact, I say to the man, that this is not a state operation, this is private enterprise. That is a tremendous responsibility! And I think, this man Henzig is perfectly right for the post, but I say: I can imagine an older man holding such a post, *but such a young man.* . . . I keep thinking: Henzig is the man for the post, yet I say: You are surely biting off more than you can chew. . . . Henzig does not answer that. Then he says that incidentally he speaks French (of course), English, Russian, and Italian. Well, I say, I cannot decide at the moment. No," the prince said, "at the moment you cannot expect a decision. I say: I'll write to you. Give me your exact address. In two days you'll receive a telegram. I stand up," the prince said, "and offer my hand to Henzig. I open the door for him, because there is no one else around to open it for him, no one, and he's gone. Henzig, no one else, I tell myself, and I think, sitting down in the office, and I think, why did the man's rightness, his general orderliness, order personified, so repel you? His education? I have to clap my hand to my head. This sudden dislike for enormous knowledge, I told myself," the prince said. "Again and again I say: A good man, a good man, what a good man this fellow Henzig is. . . . I pace back and forth in the office. I reckon out the spring income from the gravel pits. I think: Are these gravel pits still profitable? While I begin to think about the large work force in the gravel pits (and in the mines) and to wonder whether I should not close the mines altogether—close them, I think, close the mines *and* the gravel pits, it's high time—there is a knock at the door and another (the third) applicant stands before me: Huber."

The prince said: "Huber is from Bundau. He uses a language, has a way of speaking, that instantly made me think: *inimical to civilization*. I think: This is a man who is glad to and not glad to leave Bundau. Or rather: who would be glad to leave Bundau if he could leave it gladly. And so on. . . . He has left Bundau; but surely not only because of the advertisement. I ask him at once: Have you left Bundau because of my advertisement? The man is out of the question, I think. He says: Because of the ad, yes. I say: But I am looking for a topnotch man. I think of Henzig. To that Huber responds that he has thirty years' experience, without saying experience in what. I look at the man and I know," the prince said, "what kind of experience the man has had for thirty years. *Foreman of a woodcutting crew*. I tell him to sit down, there's a chair, and Huber sits. Grotesque! I pour him a glass of whisky and again I say: I don't drink, myself, on doctor's orders, but talking is easier over a drink. Huber drinks his glass down at one swig. Grotesque! His clothes are neat; they are hung on a nail, not in a closet, I think. I pour him another. I look at his hat, his jacket, his trousers, his coat buttons. I think: It's cold in Bundau, the winter never ends there, the people who live in Bundau are absolute winter people. Subsistence farmers, I think, Doctor, subsistence people. It's an area that permits a bare minimum subsistence. The prevailing tone there is blackish green, a greenish blackness, a darkness so great it actually prevents suicides. In these people thought is perpetually on the verge of drowning, any pleasure in life on the verge of perishing, everything freezes and dies. Why, how are things in Bundau nowadays? I ask Huber. Always the same, Huber says. Several times, Doctor, he repeats: Always the same. Drack, the sawmill owner, lives in Bundau, doesn't he? I say. Oh yes,

Drack, the sawmill owner, Huber says. I say: It was Drack who made the floors for the Belvedere, wasn't it? I say: Drack has three sisters. It's a pleasure talking to Drack, I say. You know," the prince said, "Drack is the only man in Bundau who has money. Yes, Huber says. I am thinking," the prince said, "that it is inexplicable that three applicants should have come in answer to my advertisement the very first morning. What do you say to that, Doctor, three applicants on the first morning to a ridiculous want-ad in a ridiculous newspaper, composed in an altogether ridiculous style? What do you say? I say to Huber," the prince said, "Drack has shifted entirely to making parquet, hasn't he? He no longer makes ordinary flooring, does he? Except occasionally, I say. There are exceptions, Huber says. I am thinking that my want-ad was badly written. Why should three applicants respond to a badly written want ad on the first morning? Mysterious. Mysterious!" the prince said. "I thought, it's not Huber's fault. Fault? Huber? Why? Stop this, I thought. I ask Huber *when* he read the advertisement," the prince said. "I certainly want to know that," the prince said. "It strikes me that I also asked Henzig and Zehetmayer about it. I say: When did you read the want ad? Do you have it there in your pocket? I say. Huber takes the advertisement out of his pocket and puts it on the desk. I read it through once more. Did you read it at breakfast, I ask. He says he did not, and indicates that he has not even had his breakfast yet," the prince said. "He succeeds in conveying that without saying a word; everything about the man suddenly tells me that he has not yet eaten breakfast. I go into the kitchen," the prince said. "I see that there is nobody in the kitchen, not a soul in the kitchen, I fix a ham sandwich and butter a roll for Huber, and go back to the office with it and tell him to eat. Cider? I ask. No, no cider. Of course he has children, but I am not sure whether there are three or four. I say, Eat! and ask: How many children do you have? Three, he says. How old, I want to know. Thirty-one, twenty-four, and sixteen, he says. Four have died. I think: What matters is life? I say: You have a fine wife, eh? She does a good job of farming eight and a half acres, Huber says," the prince said. "If it weren't for Drack, Drack in Bundau. He nods. Drack, I say, indirectly feeds Bundau. Drack philosophizes and his three sisters keep him well-stuffed, which he hates, I say. It's tough sledding with three sisters, I say. Drack and Bundau . . ." the prince said. "And then it occurs to me: You have two sisters in the house yourself. It also occurs to me that I'm the same age as Drack. And it occurs to me that basically the same conditions exist in Drack's house as in mine, the economic, familial, and personal circumstances, only Drack is *down* and I'm *up,* but I could just as well be down and Drack up. . . . I say to Huber," the prince said. "But Drack's sisters are hunchbacks, and I think that Drack is the victim of his three sisters. A man can be strong, as strong as he likes, and Drack is strong, but his three sisters are stronger. . . . Unmarried Drack is a result, I think; widowed Saurau is a result. I say: Drack could have made a dozen good matches. I say this more to myself than to Huber, but Huber hears it," the prince said, "and he stops eating and says: The Princess of Thurn and Taxis. Afterward Huber says that hoof-and-mouth disease in Bundau has finished off almost all the livestock, that Bundau will never recover again. Do you hear that, Doctor, never *recover* again! Epidemics, I say, once they come, it's too late.

For the state, I say, everything is too late. For the kind of state we have nowadays, everything is always too late. The state wastes medicines on carcasses! Well, I say, when did you read the want ad, Huber? His wife brought the newspaper back with her from Knittelfeld very early in the morning. Gone there to consult the doctor," the prince said. "Kidney disease. Huber took the newspaper from her while he was putting on his shirt. She'd been nagging him as she did every day, saying they had no money. *He* didn't work, *she* worked her fingers to the bone, *he* idled, earned nothing, *she* was keeping everything going, *he* squandered everything, and so on. . . . Finally she called him a layabout and a shirker, and then he lost his temper," the prince said, "and threatened to slap her, but didn't do so and went into the bedroom and threw himself down on the bed. I read the want ad there on the bed, Huber said. He had immediately jumped up and dressed and left the house and come from Bundau to see me. On the way it had struck him as foolish to apply for the position (Zehetmayer!). But no, he had kept telling himself, I'll go up there, I'll go up, I'll go up to see Prince Saurau. And what with repeating to himself, I'mgoingup, I'mgoingup, he suddenly found himself up on top. But the sight of the castle disheartened him, he said, and he walked around it four or five times before he knocked. Again and again he wondered whether he shouldn't run off, down to a tavern. . . . But then he saw Henzig coming out, *a rather impressive man,* said Huber, and there was nothing left for him to do but knock. At my age it would be foolish to start in on a new job, Huber said to me. But his wife was constantly after him," the prince said, "she was driving him crazy. Every day she proved to him *her indispensability and his superfluousness.* But of course he wasn't at all suited to the post he was applying for, Huber said, and by that he meant not entirely unsuited—probably. It occurs to me that the abilities of a foreman are first-rate," the prince said. "Huber's abilities are probably the finest, and I say so. I say: Your abilities are undoubtedly excellent. But he might also be thinking that he was not suited to the post of steward, I said. No, no, I say," the prince said, "such a post calls for a quite different sort of experience. He knows that, and I say candidly not that Huber is *probably not* suited to the post, but that he is *simply unsuited* for it. I say," the prince said, "but it would surely be a blessing to get away from Bundau again. Yes, Huber said. I myself have not been in Bundau for two years," the prince said. "As usual it is only a funeral that prompts me to leave the castle, to visit valleys. I'm constantly going to all sorts of regions in the country (and abroad too, of course) because someone dies whom I'm related to, whom I know or don't know. People of our sort are always travelers to funerals, in addition to our regular occupations. And the ones who die, Doctor, are always those whom we expected to die. Surprises are rare. I say," the prince said, "the cemetery in Bundau is being enlarged, isn't it? And Huber says: Disputes. The mayor, the socialists . . . and so on. . . . Nobody wanted to give up any land for the town, Huber says. So the town simply expropriated some. Expropriated, I think. For me that is a cue that brings to mind the whole repulsiveness of the state, the stupidity of the state, the whole idiotic bureaucratic rabble who run the state. Expropriated! Everywhere there are expropriations, I say; everywhere down below me land is being expropriated for the most paltry reasons. The politicians expropriate here and there.

Everywhere. They expropriate and they ruin. Nature is being ruined. Expropriated! I cry out, and I say: I hope this state expropriates itself soon. I hope it commits suicide as fast as possible, I cry! It's high time for this Republic to expropriate itself!" the prince said. "This ridiculous Republic, I said. Expropriated! They hack off your toes, Doctor, they cut off toes and heels. Nobody can walk any more! Suddenly," the prince said—we had stood still and were gazing down into the gorge—"suddenly I've poured Huber another glass of whisky and am in the midst of talking politics with him. The state is rotten, I say, in all seriousness the Republic is rotting. That is my favorite phrase of late, Doctor: *The state is rotten*. Everything is empty, I say to Huber: The Reds are empty and the Blacks are empty, the monarchy is empty of course, and of course the Republic is empty. After all, everything is lying dully, lethargically in its death-throes, right? Everything except for science. I say to Huber: The republican death-throes are probably the most repulsive, the ugliest of all. Aren't they, Doctor? I say: The common people are stupid, they stink, and that has always been so. Huber says then that there are Communists in Bundau, and what is more among Drack's workers. Communists! I say. Communists! Yes, Communists. There are plenty of them working for me as well, I say. Everybody down below the castle is communistic, I say. Everybody. But the Communists don't know what Communism is. Unfortunately! Then, coming back to my want ad, I say to Huber that he, Huber, is undoubtedly a good man, but as I've said, unsuited for the post of steward." The prince said he thought the man was fifty but he looked sixty. "Fifty years ago it would have been perfectly possible to consider a foreman for such a post," the

prince said. "But not nowadays. Nowadays the business requires a scientific type, like Henzig. No, I say to Huber, after
all you did not seriously think that I could employ you! Half
past eleven, Huber, I say," the prince said. "I pour a fourth
glass for him. I say: The man you saw going out, the good-
looking man, he's the one. Henzig, I say, he's the one. Forestry school, I say, soil culture, Vienna, Paris, London, Madrid.
And a robust body besides, as I said, I say. English, French,
Italian . . . Kobernausserwald, I say. Has that modern arro-
gance and scientific attitude, unsparing even toward himself.
Those scientists aren't stupid people, I say. Basically it seems
to me," the prince said, "forestry today is simply an economic
science, if not a pure natural science. Everything is a science
today, I say," the prince said. "Huber wants to stand up, but
doesn't. Everything is a gigantic scientific apparatus, I say.
Absurd, I say. Huber stands up. In Austria, I say to Huber,
everything is bogged down in a perverse backwardness. Two
hundred years behind the times in almost all fields, I say.
Ridiculous, I say. That isn't any exaggeration, Doctor, and I
say: Substances, I say, a mighty chemistry. The farther away
it moves from the conventional concept of nature, the more
beautiful, the mightier, I want even to say, the more poetic.
Huber, I say, how is the mail delivery in Bundau nowadays?
Still a ghastly mess, Huber says, ghastly. And the schoolchildren? I ask. Without further words, by merely saying
*schoolchildren* I summon to mind all my concern for the
misery of the schoolchildren in the mountain districts.
Huber goes to the door," the prince said. "I think: His trousers, absurd. His jacket, absurd. His walk, absurd. Grotesque, I think. The concept of schoolchildren, Doctor, is
equivalent to misery throughout the world, but in the Bun-

dau region the situation is the worst, the bitterest it can be anywhere. For twenty years there has been talk about building a new school at the end of the Bundau valley, but to this day no new school has been built. I think repeatedly: The whole educational system in our country is backward, simply outmoded, wretched, isn't it, Doctor? And I think: If you allow every sudden inspiration to coagulate into a thought. . . . I say: Huber, one must not *reflect*. . . . I have been reflecting, Doctor, on the stupidity of all phrases, on stupidity, on the stupidity in which man lives and thinks, thinks and lives, on the stupidity. . . . I permit myself to live—absurd! Everyone lives—absurd. The stupidity of entrusting oneself to the German language, my dear Doctor—absurd! And not only the German language, I think, but still the German language above all. The stupidity resulting from German, I think. . . . The stupidity of a world consisting of advantage and disadvantage and of nothing else. . . . Philosophize! No! In Bundau I once saw a plump pheasant sitting on a boar, I say to Huber. I really did. Huber listens. Listen, Doctor, Huber listens. . . . He is standing at the door. Yes, yes, I say, I went down into Bundau hundreds of times with my father, for the pheasants and the boars, I say. Bundau kept drawing my father into it—the attraction of Bundau, I say. I was perhaps eight or nine years old, I say, when we went to Bundau, very early in the morning, and suddenly deep in the valley we saw the pheasant sitting on the boar. Then my father described to me the relationship between the pheasant and the boar. Grotesque! I say. And he told me all sorts of things about pheasants and boars. We were sitting on a log, my father and I, and as the pheasant shamelessly bobbed up and down on the boar's tail, my father shot it. Shot it right off the boar's tail, I say. The boar takes one leap and disappears into the underbrush. I go after the pheasant, and while I am stooping for it my father fires a second shot. I ask him as I come back with the pheasant why he fired the second shot. Into the air, I say, why into the air? My father doesn't know why. I've never fired a shot pointlessly into the air, my father says. There are fine pheasants and fine boars in Bundau, I say. Huber wants to leave. He steps into the vestibule. Of course, I say, I can use you, though not for the steward's post. I propose to Huber that he work for me as foreman, though without old-age pension; Krainer needs help. But he doesn't accept my offer. A queer man. It's clear that Huber doesn't want to work, not any more, never again. No, no, he says. He would rather go on listening to his wife's nagging every day. I think: Huber would be a real help to me. You see, everything is neglected, Doctor. But it's no use, Huber leaves. I reflect that my want ad has helped him escape from Bundau. Cold Bundau, I think. Huber as steward, I think. Huber and Zehetmayer—grotesque! I'll settle with Henzig at once, I think. Henzig is the only fellow for the job. Basically Henzig is what I have always been looking for and never found. I realize," the prince said, "that there is a personality who in no time will become priceless, indispensable to me. The man is first-rate. Of course it takes a whole day," the prince said, "for the telegram to reach Kobernausserwald. If I send it now, at noon, I thought, it won't reach Kobernausserwald until tomorrow morning. The postal system, the hopeless, ruined Austrian postal system. I go into the vestibule and dictate the telegram to my elder sister, and she calls old Krainer and he rides down to the post office. I'm not running any risks with Hen-

zig," the prince said. "I've already settled the financial side
with him. He'll live in the hunting lodge, no, in the Pavilion,
no, in the hunting lodge, in the hunting lodge. *Assume du-
ties of position at once if you wish,* I telegraphed. But it occurs to me that Henzig is still under contract to the state and
can't begin work until next week at the earliest. The state
forests which ruin everything," Prince Saurau said, "the state
which ruins everything, the unending, everlasting suicide of
the state. Doctor, nowadays all states are constantly commit-
ting suicide, and not only in Europe. It is my ancient theme,
Doctor," the prince said. "The state that ruins everything,
the people who do not know how to run their state and ruin
it. The phrase *intellectual catastrophe* occurs to me, Doctor.
After Huber has left, I have a sign reading *Steward's position filled* put up on the big gate, and go into the office. And
sure enough, a number of other applicants for the job arrive.
I watch them until they leave, some immediately after reading the sign, most after hesitating for quite a while. Much
too old. Again and again I wonder that so many applicants
should respond to this particular want ad. Remarkable, I
think, that the right man was among the first three applicants, isn't it, Doctor? To talk with people one has just met
makes you thoughtful and is very tiring. There is always the
question of how much one should make contact with them,
whether one should make contact with them at all. Doctor,
don't you think . . . contacts," the prince said. "As you always say, Doctor: I *am* insofar as I have contact with people,
and so on. But contact always brings out first of all the ironic
element in my mind. . . . Irony, which diminishes the unbearableness. . . . Brushing against the peripheries of people with weak nerves. . . . I think: Was I too friendly with

Huber, or was I not friendly enough with Huber? And
how was I toward Zehetmayer? Odd that the question of
whether I was too friendly or too unfriendly always arises as
soon as a person has left me. But I was quite friendly toward
Huber, I think. And I was also quite friendly toward
Zehetmayer. I certainly was least friendly with Henzig. It
was a very short interview, an encounter, a surge of dislike
for the man. Henzig, I think, is the ideal steward."

Even among his sisters and daughters, Prince Saurau
went on to say, when he could no longer bear to stay in his
room and went down into the lower rooms "hoping for the
relief of conversation," to find them sitting in "the dusk that
always reigns in Hochgobernitz," either chatting or silently
"contemplating themselves in preparation for the night"—
even among them he more and more heard the noises that he
had often told my father about. For months these noises had
not left him, he said.

Devoting more and more of his intellectual capacities "to
the higher exaltation and the higher speculation" (Father's
phrase), in his weaknesses, even in that condition which in
the course of the past several months had become an excruci-
ating torment, when he locked himself in his room to conduct, alone with himself, his "masochistic discussions" (Father's phrase), which he continued even during his son's stay
in England and which, probably due to the fact that he was
doomed to stay on in Hochgobernitz to the end of his days,
he conducted with utter ruthlessness chiefly toward himself,
pitching them at such a level, in spite of the extreme irritabil-
ity from which he suffered, as to require the utmost tension
of his mind, an ever-increasing ruthless tension of his mental
powers. "Consistently delving into all scientific phenomena"

(Saurau's phrase), he had heard these "fatal noises" (Father's phrase) even in the course of last night while he was studying Cardinal Retz's memoirs, had "been forced to hear them," though he was no longer able to remember at what point in time these noises had imposed themselves upon him. He now heard them continually, he said, and could no longer fall asleep; he feared these noises more and more. Day and night in the past week these noises had penetrated his consciousness, deranged him, constantly and in the cruelest manner "projected" him into his own death.

The terrible part of it was that to the very degree that he thought he had to withdraw from the world, he was falling prey to it, Prince Saurau said. "We think fantastically and are weary," he said. In "the drive to exhaust all possibilities" he had cast a pall of gloom over Hochgobernitz, and Hochgobernitz over him. "The analogies are deadly" had by now become one of his recurrent, decisive phrases.

Saurau spoke of his family as "this continual, outrageous truncation of the mind." They were ruling here in Hochgobernitz in his name. "With the hapless impotence for which they are made they inhale their daily life primarily into their bodies and secondarily into their heads in the form of hundreds and thousands of dismaying intellectual kleptomanias, from the greatest remove." Meanwhile he, Prince Saurau, in the midst of them, in the midst of their "catastrophic company," was being plagued by these noises ("rumblings in the earth?" [Father's phrase]). Feeling his brain ("irruption of water into what has been parched from time immemorial?" [Saurau's phrase]) painfully as a membrane abused in behalf of all mankind, knowing these noises to have existed always in humanity ("a transformation of what is into something else that will be" [Saurau's phrase]), he no longer merely heard these noises, but also saw and felt them in his head. His brain must suffer these noises ("expanding fault lines, an ideal disintegrative process in nature!"). He found himself suddenly and uncontrollably injecting all sorts of phrases into his torment, and almost all of them ended with "for the sake of all mankind."

He often felt, he said, the vast span of "emotional and geological history coalescing into wholly new substances," which he regarded as a process in which "everything is destroyed in order ultimately to become."

"Here, on this spot, I always would discuss everything concerning Hochgobernitz with my steward," Prince Saurau said, and he called our attention to broad areas in the valley that had been devastated by the flood that recently affected a great part of the countryside below Hochgobernitz. "No more than three weeks ago," Prince Saurau said, "I was walking up and down here, shocked beyond words by this tremendous flood damage. And while I was watching the slow recession of the water, silent, horrified, in a state of derangement that lasted for two hours, Doctor," he began to think about the dubious life of his son, who was studying in England. "On this spot," Prince Saurau said, "I always think about my son. The fact is that my son's life is completely estranged from mine." From this spot three weeks ago he had watched the receding high waters and then "without saying a single word against nature," returned to the castle. Now he said: "My son is in England and I am going under here."

At his last visit, my father recalls, Prince Saurau, commenting on the flood, kept exclaiming "landslide" and spoke of "despair assailing his mind." Again and again he exclaimed "landslide" and kept reckoning "flood damage, flood costs, flood sums." The whole region was afflicted by a mild but "insidious" smell of decaying cadavers—on both banks of the Ache a great many drowned cattle had been wedged against houses and trees, torn open, bloated, some "dismembered by the power of the water" (my father), and many head of livestock from the Saurau barns in the valley had not yet been cleared away. And because of this smell the prince had kept exclaiming words like *decay, dissolution,* and the word *diluvianism.* Then he had suddenly declared that the noises in his brain were wreaking far greater devastation inside his head than what could be seen on the banks of the Ache down below. "Here in my head," Saurau had said, "there is actually *inconceivable devastation.*"

This first day after the flood seems to my father to have been a critical one for the prince's illness, which then evolved "at a furious rate" (Father). "On that day both of us, horrified by the extent of the catastrophe, went down to the Ache," Father said. Actually, the extent of the flood, as they both observed after the water had receded to its normal level, had indeed been catastrophic. Prince Saurau seemed to find it incomprehensible that the flood should have happened immediately after the steward's death. "Right now, when I'm completely without help!" he had exclaimed again and again. At first the two of them had been so shocked by the sight that they had not been able to say a word to one another, although they had no doubt greeted the workmen who were busy dragging wood and corpses out of the water. They had tried to walk as far as possible; the prince had begged my father not to cut his visit as short as he customarily did, because he could not stand being alone. Again and again Prince Saurau had spoken of "damage in the millions," my father said. And after remaining silent for hours during their inspection tour, the prince talked without a stop once they were back at the castle.

Prince Saurau now said to me: "The more intensively I talked about the flood, the more your father was distracted from the flood. Moreover," the prince said, "he was distracted by the play that was put on in the pavilion the day before the terrible flood. This play, a different one every year," Prince Saurau said, "is a tradition at Hochgobernitz. The curious thing is," Saurau said, "and I am speaking now of an absurdity that is absolutely phenomenal: The moment I began talking about the flood, your father began talking about the play. The more I was preoccupied with the flood, the more preoccupied your father became with the play. I talked about the flood and he talked about the play."

My father said: "I kept thinking all along that you couldn't help talking about the flood, but I talked about the play."

Prince Saurau said: "But I talked about the flood and not about the play, for what else could I possibly have talked about that day, if not the flood! Naturally I could not think of anything but the flood. And your father thought of nothing but the play. As I became more and more preoccupied with the flood, your father became more and more preoccupied with the play, and insofar as I, speaking of the flood, was irritated by your father's speaking of the play, your father, speaking of the play, was irritated by me because I spoke of nothing but the flood. There was tremendous irritation!" the prince said. "Again and again I heard your father commenting on the play in the midst of my endless talk about the flood. The incredible, amazing thing was," the prince said, "that as the time went on I spoke more and more about the flood and nothing else and your father spoke about the play and nothing else. And your father spoke more and more loudly about the play, and I more and more loudly about the flood. Loudly, equally loudly, at the same time, both of us, your father and I went on, he speaking about a tremendous play, I about a tremendous flood. And then," the prince said, "there came a period in which both of us spoke exclusively about the flood, followed by a period in which we talked of nothing but the play. But while we were both talking about the play, I was thinking only about the flood, and while we were talking about the flood, your father was thinking only of the play; while your father thought of the play, my thoughts were with the flood. If we talked about the flood, I thought that your father wanted to talk about the play; if we talked about the play, I wanted to talk about nothing but the flood."

"I wanted to compare the play," my father said, "with a play I once saw in Oxford, and to discuss the qualities of English actors versus the qualities of our actors, as well as the difference between the English language and ours."

The prince said: "Naturally I was completely obsessed with the flood, but your father was just as naturally *not* obsessed with the play."

"When we talked about the play," my father said, "you, Prince, kept exclaiming *What expense!* or *Enormous expense!* while I, whenever we talked about the flood, was constantly using such words as *stage machinery, pantomime, dramatic climax, puppetry.*"

"But basically," the prince said, "no matter what we talked about on that day, we were really talking about nothing but the flood."

"Immediately after the play," the prince said, "I left the pavilion and walked on the inner walls, because despite the play my mind had not been rid of the noises. And I had been hoping particularly that the play would distract me from my noises. But in fact I could not find distraction from the noises on the inner walls either, and I went to the outer walls. For a short time on the outer walls it was possible for me to shake off the noises, and I looked down from the outer wall at the people who had come to the play and were now riding home. Some went down into the gorge," the prince said. "I can't imagine what for. To this day I don't know why some went down into the gorge. Standing behind a large hemlock, I watched the people bidding good-by to my sisters and my daughters. This play," the prince said to me, "is arranged by the women, of course. I really have nothing to do with the whole business, but the women put on such a play every year. They invite hundreds of people, people wholly uninteresting to me, and the majority of them repulsive. For the women the play, of course, is always a pretext to invite hundreds of people, who actually come, but then again the play is the least of the reasons for their coming," the prince said. "The women merely use it to bring the people to the castle, and the people who come up to the castle for the play do not come on account of the play, but out of sheer curiosity. If it were up to me," the prince said, "not a soul would come up here any more, not a soul, not a single person. I grant you," he said, "such solitariness is a morbid state, of course. But society, and I mean the whole of society, but in particular the social class that comes to the play, consists of a despicable rabble. But I let the women have their pleasure, and they can invite whomever they like. Since I don't want to see anyone at Hochgobernitz, the play is a horror to me. Actually," the prince said, "I stood behind the big hemlock for a few minutes without hearing any noises at all. But in order to warm up, for I had the feeling I was freezing, I walked partway across the courtyard, finally ran a short way, and then, walking slowly, I repeated inaudibly several sentences from the play. My memory has not yet been destroyed, I thought, no, my memory is still intact, since I am able to recite whole sentences from the play, and what is more the most complicated ones. As I walked across the yard, declaiming sentences from the play, I thought that the women and also the young Pole, a relative of ours, had already gone to bed. I actually took pleasure in declaiming whole parts of the play, the longest roles, without a single mistake. Whole sections," the prince said, "refreshing myself in the rhythm of the sentences. For over an hour I walked back and forth in the courtyard, once on the inner walls, once on the outer walls, without noticing where I was while I walked, and recalled to memory as much as possible of the text of the play. It actually is a good play, it seems to me," the prince said, "written by one of my cousins, solely for this one performance. I tested my memory in the most ruthless way," the prince said. "I did not spare myself, and I discovered that my memory is intact. Actually, Doctor, my memory was intact that evening. Suddenly it was absolutely intact. I reconstructed the play," the prince said. "I was particularly interested in its innermost construction. The theatrical aspects. Suddenly," the prince said, "I had the feeling that I could go to sleep, that feeling which has become utterly foreign to me, and I descended from the inner wall where I happened to be and went into the yard and started for my room. At first I did not intend to pass through the library, but then I went through the library anyhow; there was a book that interested me, and I wanted to start on it," the prince said. "And as I entered the library," he said, "I found the women. I was astonished that they were still up. The Polish cousin was there too. The whole company was sitting on the floor. It was four o'clock in the morning, I saw. The whole company was oddly motionless, sitting on cushions on the floor. There they sat, dead tired on their cushions, in a kind of sleepless tension, with their whisky. Suddenly," the prince said, "I had the greatest desire to start a discussion with these people. 'Isn't it cold here?' I said to them. 'Isn't it much too cold here?' And I started at once talking about the antibody in nature. The subject sprang to my mind at once. I was able to develop my thoughts in the early morning chill very well and very rapidly," the prince said. "I had good listeners; suddenly I felt: You haven't had such good listeners in a long time, you've waited for years for such good listeners. To think that these people can listen so well! And also discuss! I thought. The young Pole discussed splendidly, splendidly," the prince said. "But all at once, and now notice this, Doctor," the prince said, "the noises came back. So all this while I have been able to suppress them only once, I thought, suppress them by means of the play. Yes, the play! The noises instantly destroyed my thoughts, changed everything inside my head into a chaos. Deafening. Naturally my listeners knew nothing about that. Naturally not," the prince said. "They couldn't look inside my brain, of course. But my lis-

teners certainly felt that a wonderful orderliness inside my
brain had suddenly become a frightful chaos, a frightful,
deafening chaos. The pain at that moment," the prince said,
"when the noises started again and shattered everything inside my brain, was so frightful that I thought I would have
to stop my lecture and therefore put an end to the whole
discussion. But because, as I've said, I had not had such atten-
tive listeners for years, such honest, exacting, and, so it
seemed to me, such highly charged listeners, so splendidly
equipped for discussion—because of this I would not give in
and succeeded in restoring order in my brain. It was half past
four in the morning and I spoke partly, because that was
requisite, in Polish; above all I had to keep my attention
fixed on the Pole. I spoke about the antibody in nature, I
spoke on nature and on the antibody in nature, on nature
and on the antibody and on the antibody that emerges *from*
nature. While working out these ideas I probed the degrees
of difficulty in my thinking contrasted with the degrees of
difficulty in the thinking of my listeners. Probably because of
the play," the prince said, "this intellectual tension among
us, which I had thought no longer possible, had suddenly
become possible again. It was like a scientific conference.
There developed an intellectual community that was the
most concentrated thing imaginable, partly because of the
Pole's presence. At the climax of the discussion I told my
listeners what a discussion is, told them that a discussion is
something entirely different from what people nowadays
think a discussion is. I had the impression that the people
assembled in the library were completely transformed, that
they were not horrible relatives, but receptive people, capable
of thought, capable of trains of thought, capable of develop-

ing trains of thought, able to engage in discussion. I found
them fundamentally changed characters," the prince said.
"They were all suddenly different! I had the impression that
I was speaking to scientific minds. Pacing back and forth, I
spoke to scientists! And all at once I myself no longer had a
chaotic mind capable of registering nothing but pain, but a
clear, scientific brain. Because my thinking was absolutely
clear, when I gave examples of it, commented on it, it was
steadily incorporated into my listeners, something I no
longer thought possible. That morning," Prince Saurau said,
"we enjoyed exercising our minds, even as we enjoyed the
dissolving night around us, the daylight coming from the
east, the tremendous mechanism of frogs and crickets re-
treating into the gorge and the valleys. While dawn broke,
we abruptly no longer felt ourselves destroyers of one another's nerves. We had reformed. In all our faces I observed
the tranquility of our feelings and mental states, for all that
it contained elements of sexual awakening. That morning I
realized that we are not yet entirely shattered. My son's sisters," the prince said, "fitted in just as well as my own sisters,
subordinated themselves to my thought, which had seemed
to all of them, *in tranquility,* a bearable and not an unbearable fantasy, because of the play. Thanks to the sudden clarity of our brains we were all suddenly moved by nature," the
prince said. "How rarely we are capable of tranquility. Suddenly we were all together capable of absorbing the tranquility that always prevails here in Hochgobernitz, and we all
felt not the slightest antipathies or weakness. Without any
one of them feeling the slightest faltering in their intellectual
capacities, they all followed the explanation (as I also was
able to observe with growing astonishment) of a monstrosity

within the universal physical and chemical machine, a monstrosity that was steadily taking possession of all of us. But all the while," the prince said, "there were those agonizing noises in my brain. While I led us with the greatest sureness through our thinking as through our own darkness, because I know it, I was constantly being distracted from life by the frightful noises in my brain. Among my own people I felt that I had long ago become invisible to all of them, and I felt so more and more. Suddenly I no longer existed for them at all, was no longer *there*. I tried to conjure up a mirror image of myself, which cost me the greatest effort, and I made them all look into this mirror image. I imagined," Prince Saurau said, "that by remaining out on the ramparts and in the yard (after the play) I would once again be able to make a thrust into life there in the library; I seized the opportunity, but in reality I did not succeed. The noises in my head thwart me completely. For a long time I have heard them redoubling every day," the prince said. "But my torment is a torment beyond your grasp," he said to my father.

My father goes to see the prince only to treat him for his insomnia, I thought, without doing anything about his real illness, without, as became more and more evident to me while we walked back and forth along the outer wall of the castle, doing anything about his madness. For suddenly I saw quite clearly that the prince is mad, which had not been evident to me while he was talking about his interviews in the morning. It had seemed then that the prince was not mad, and when he spoke about the applicants for the post of steward I had thought that the prince was anything but mad, contrary to my father's remarks, for my father in the past had always called the prince mad. But now, as we walked faster and faster on the outer walls of the castle, I saw that the prince *is* actually mad.

The prince said: "The difficulty that morning, Doctor, the morning after the play, was for me this: From the moment I entered the library, saw my relatives sitting on the floor, and became aware that I must lead the discussion, must deliver a lecture, I knew that now I could no longer turn back. Now I can no longer return to my thinking, isolated as it is in my thousands of principles. I cannot simply return to my own brain. I must think *aloud,* must publicly establish clarity about so completely linear a matter as the problem of the antibody in nature. For it is linear, even though it is highly complicated and possibly insoluble. But along with this, Doctor, I must, as an artificial human sacrifice, balance upon a rope stretched across the entire world of the mind, across all sciences and arts, causes and effects, must pass through past and future millennia, through all the innumerable concepts of nature, with my brain presumably already far out in the universal atmosphere, and must move, balancing on my rope, toward a goal lying in uttermost darkness, a goal from which an icy chill already wafted toward me."

We stood still.

"Such a night as the night after the play, the play was good, Doctor, it was a very good play," the prince said, "such a tranquil night, this calm before the flood, Doctor (because of the play), one of those quiet nights which have become very rare in Hochgobernitz—you can imagine how rare these quiet nights have become in Hochgobernitz since my son has been gone—because the quiet is perfect in Hochgobernitz, because it is really all there is, there is not quiet any more. . . . There simply is no more quiet, no peace, no tran-

quility in Hochgobernitz. That night and that cold morning
among us and among the books, in this icy cold daybreak
atmosphere in which feelings freely are transmuted into
thoughts and thoughts freely transmuted into feelings, and
that is the ideal magic suddenly to be together and find one
another bearable—that night, in which the self-destructive
and self-disintegrating elements of the family were so clev-
erly muted, whether from weariness *after* the play or from
madness *before* the dawn, or from madness and weariness
*after* the play *and* before the dawn, so that suddenly in truth
everything was able to exist and everything was justified in
existing—imagine, suddenly everybody in the house felt the
prevailing quiet in the house merely as a quiet prevailing in
the house; the dreadfulness of it, the uncanniness of it, had
suddenly been taken away. A suddenly uninstrumental society constituted directly for evil, quite in the nature of this
house, a society in which a day shaken by the play was transformed from philosophical and unbearable to nonphilosoph-
ical and bearable (perhaps a brilliant compound!). On this
morning in which the autumn for the first time became pal-
pable in me, in me and, differently, in the others—we
suddenly were able to look within ourselves into this year's
autumn (each of us into his own autumn), look in because
of our excitement before the play and during the play, look
into the tranquility of the autumn after the play, by means of
our inner geometry look into the perishing of outer nature."

On the morning after the play, with all of them assembled in the library—"except for my son nearly all the members of the family were assembled there," the prince said, *"all
of them,"* he repeated, and added that for many years he had
not observed all of them assembled in Hochgobernitz—on

that morning after the play he had delivered a "dissecting lecture," he said. "They all sit there and listen to what I have to say about nature, and hear about the concept of nature and the concept of the antibody in nature, about the antibody nature concept, and I suddenly find myself looking into my family, into a monstrously large, monstrously outmoded Hochgobernitz, into a horrifying history growing increasingly sinister as it recedes back toward its origins, into a ghastly stench of generations, into a more and more stinking art of generations, artificiality of generations, into a labyrinth of dead horror stories under the Saurau name, from which from time to time I actually keep hearing cries of horror, Doctor, I actually hear cries of horror coming up out of the labyrinth of my family, the belated cries of horror of those who died before me. . . . Yes," the prince said, "my son doesn't write to me, my son is silent, my son studies silently in England, my silently studying son in England. He writes no letters of truth."

And a few steps farther on the prince said: "The flood is costing me one and a half millions. A flood in the millions. But," he said, reverting to the morning after the play, "as I stood there among my people, among those who had remained with me in Hochgobernitz, and as I explained everything to them, but chiefly to this Pole with the highly intelligent face, explained nature, and explained the nature of explanation, for all explanation must be explained," the prince said, "that's an ancient, necessary process, well then, as I was attempting to explain and throw light on the concept of nature, the twilight of dawn helps me enormously, the sharpness of the air—as I was talking I look into the faces of my sisters and my daughters—in this autumnal cold one suddenly sees very acutely, Doctor—and I see them all together, I also see my son, my absent son, Doctor, see them all together through myself, and a monstrous constellation dawns on me, possibly the one concept that is sheer horror in itself: *I am the father!*"

The prince said: "I see all of them as an incredibly differentiated proto-reality, this proto-reality which comes from me and from which I come—and in my brain there is the din of the noises."

Far off, down in the valley, as if in a marionette theater worked from below, we saw laborers on a wooden bridge obeying an invisible foreman, and in the sudden chill in the air we heard a rapidly accelerating din of noises rising up through the woods.

The prince said: "I have the impression that it would be natural for the world to fly apart at any moment. Or is it that nature must destroy herself?" he said. "This process is always one that proceeds from within and completes itself outwardly. When I come to, am forced to, this observation, this view, because I apparently have an organism geared only for this observation, this view—when I come to it, I have the feeling that the time has arrived—at first it is only a crumbling, cracks, tears, a rending and crumbling! . . . This time can go on for centuries, of course, centuries behind me, centuries before me. Millennia. But what astounds me," the prince said, "is not the fact that these noises have been in my brain, that these noises are always there, have always been, always will be, but the horrible fact that no human being with whom I have ever come in contact—and, my dear Doctor, I have come in contact with so many people, with so many characters that if you saw them all in a heap in front of you your whole world would instantly collapse, for I've had so tremendously large a selection of humanity at my disposal and at certain times have associated every day with all possible characters and mentalities—but what astounds me, I say, is that no person, not a single brain, has ever taken notice of these noises or ever will. The fact that this is so is not so shocking, only that I alone am the one person, that my brain alone is the one brain, which is forced to note the frightfulness, the deadliness! Everyone around me—and it is always from myself, from my brain as a kind of thinking Hochgobernitz, so to speak, from my immediate surroundings, that I draw conclusions about the whole, about the whole world in which at any rate the whole of humanity has room—everyone around me has a numbing incapacity for perception, incapacity for observation, incapacity for receptivity. . . . To me this fact is deadly, it is a deadly fact to me that I am alone in this fact, *that I am alone in this fact.* This enormous landslide!" the prince cried out, and repeated several times: "This enormous landslide!"

He told us to look down into the valley at the workmen dangling from the wooden bridge. "I have to pay for all these people sitting around doing nothing, I have to pay for them. I pay these people for a disability of nature, for a disability of nature I pay all these useless people!" It seemed to me that the tone in which he says the word *people* indicates an enormous aloofness from people.

"In the past," the prince continued, "in the past, I had difficulty, just as you do, Doctor, in probing and mastering a single subject within a single problem, in penetrating the perilously varied heights and depths of a single aspect of a single train of thought; but those difficulties now seem to me insignificant compared to the state of absolute necessity in which I am now forced to operate in the greatest imaginable number of simultaneous areas in order to make any sense at all. And it is horribly plain that no limits exist any more for those areas, for as far as I am concerned I have truly arrived at the point where limitlessness has become a certainty. I have reached the permanent derangement of advanced age, the more and more philosophical, philosophistic isolation of the mind: the point where everything is continually present in consciousness, where the brain as such no longer exists. . . . The truth is that I more and more believe I am everything, because in reality I am no longer anything, and in consequence I can only feel everything human, everything humanly possible, as shameful. After the play I became fully conscious of this state in relation principally to my relatives, those relatives whom I have always called incapable of perception. More clearly than ever before I became aware of a tremendous remoteness and alienation, which simultaneously is the greatest possible closeness and comradeship in suffering, but not a comradeship in torment. I have always shared suffering with other people, but never torment. It seems to me that throughout my life I have continually had only one single thought: What potentialities for unremitting effort there are in the human mind! And I have long thought," the prince said, "that what I am immersed in is nothing but torment, a torment that is my own, that belongs only to me, that is inherent in my nature, that is my own nature, already removed from the human capacity for suffering, matured out of it, matured out of all human potentialities. Here in Hochgobernitz, where everything of late has given me continual pain, it has seemed quite natural that this thin air of the heights should be so destructive. Yet if I were but a generation back, or had a different sort of brain, I too would be fundamentally incapable of perception like the others. For a long time the realization of that fact has been a source of the deepest torment to me, and simultaneously of the greatest pleasure."

From the outer wall we went to the inner wall. The prince pointed out that in the course of only thirty years he had been able to double the property he inherited from his father, "contrary to all rumors," he said, "contrary to the whole political development in Europe, to the development of the whole world." All his life, he said, he had thought about enlarging Hochgobernitz, and one day he had observed that Hochgobernitz had in fact been doubled in size. "But my son," he said, "will destroy Hochgobernitz as soon as he receives it into his hands."

Last night, the prince said, he had had a dream. "In this dream," he said, "I was able to look at a sheet of paper moving slowly from far below to high up, paper on which my own son had written the following. I see every word that my son is writing on that sheet of paper," the prince said. "It is my son's hand writing it. My son writes: As one who has taken refuge in scientific allegories I seemed to have cured myself of my father for good, as one cures oneself of a contagious disease. But today I see that this disease is an elemental, shattering fatal illness of which everyone without exception dies. Eight months after my father's suicide—note that, Doctor, after his father's suicide, after my suicide; my son writes about my suicide!—eight months after my father's suicide everything is already ruined, and I can say that I have ruined it. I can say that I have ruined Hochgobernitz, my son writes, and he writes: I have ruined this flourishing economy! This tremendous, *anachronistic* agricultural and forest economy. I suddenly see, my son writes," the prince said, "that by liquidating the business even though or precisely because it is the best, I am for the first time implementing my theory, my son writes!" the prince said. "I have taken my first steps in reality, my son writes. From the office I see Moser coming, he writes (Moser is the town clerk); the man I hate is approaching, my son writes. I tell myself: I know what he wants, but he might want something else, but no, he is trying it for the third time. This is the third time I have observed Moser, my son writes," the prince said. "From the window of the office, with the fog gone, that utterly London-like English fog, I can now see down to the woods. I see the whole area outside the window and all the way down to the woods when I look out, and it is a looking out against my personal elemental fear, my son writes. In reality, he writes, possibly due to my even more heightened antipathy against myself ever since my return from England and against everything else, and due also to my more or less catastrophic though fantastic solitude, and likewise to my base fear of suddenly being surprised by that intruder Moser, possibly also due to a frightful situation that I am afraid of—the drastic changes within the briefest time in my physical and mental state—due to all this, my son writes, not a minute passes without my looking out of the window. Or at least every two or three minutes I look out of the window and survey the fields, and I try to determine whether anything is moving in the woods. For it often happens, my son writes, that somebody is hiding in the woods, forcing himself to immobility among the trees, out of sheer cunning; but as soon as he thinks himself unobserved he moves swiftly and with incredible speed toward his victim. Actually, my son writes, Town Clerk Moser must have been standing immobile among the trees for some time. Everything about him as he trotted across the fields toward the castle indicated that a period of time had passed, and naturally it is connected with his intentions and therefore with me; he gave himself time to think out a plan which concerns me and of course is harmful to me. . . . From the first moment I saw him, my son writes, this man has been suspect, suspect, and less because of his repulsive physical appearance than because of his base cast of mind, in which all the nastiness of his disgusting categories seemed to come together in a single, continuous evil dangerous to everyone. The man is a constant, disgusting outrage—listen, Doctor, to what my son writes. He writes: For my father this man did not exist at all (actually he is an excellent man because he is endowed with a dismal despicableness in the most dreaded sense; at every moment his physiognomy gave the lie on every count to the entire world of humanity); but I have managed to escape entirely the impact of this habitual criminal who has run around at liberty all his life, who has never come into conflict with the law and never will because the world is too stupid. I actually watched Moser long before he emerged from the woods, listen, Doctor, listen, and I even know precisely, my son writes, that he appeared at the very moment in today's reading that I had come to that dangerous agitating sentence which says that *in bourgeois revolutions bloodshed, terror, and political assassination are the indispensable weapons in the hands of the rising classes.* I saw Moser emerge from among the pine trunks in one of the most rapid movements the eye can possibly observe, and then, after two or three minutes, when I looked out of the window again as is my habit, I suddenly see him crossing the meadow, coming along the outer wall of the castle. I recognized him at once as Town Clerk Moser, and I say to myself: *Vulgar motion in itself.* I stand up, my son writes, and go into the vestibule and close the front door which I had left open because it had suddenly turned warm, but probably left open too long anyhow because it was suddenly cold again; in this house you have to be very sensitive about when to open the doors and windows and when to close them again, so that it is neither too warm nor too cold, and every window and every door demands a different rhythm of opening and shutting," the prince said, "and the weather here, I see, is unlike the weather in England, changing completely every hour, it could certainly drive you out of your mind if you plunged too deeply into this absolutely unlearnable science. Even as I closed the front door, my son writes," the prince said, "disturbed in my reading as I was, wrenched out of it, I suddenly no longer knew what was the point of the sentence which after my fashion I had multiplied and divided again about a hundred times, or the second sentence which I had repeated loudly and clearly: *The proletarian revolution needs no terrorism to accomplish its aims, for it despises killing people—* even as I closed the door I thought that I would not admit the Town Clerk Moser. I draw the curtains, my son writes," the prince said. "After all, I might be away, he writes, and he writes: I actually draw the curtains, but then open them again because it seems to me ridiculous that I should draw them on account of Town Clerk Moser. After all, I think, has Town Clerk Moser already so much power over a Saurau that I have to make any pretenses for his benefit? To make any pretenses to him and to myself? To have to draw the curtains to shut him out, close the door to shut him out . . . and I draw the curtains open again as far as possible and return to the vestibule and open the door as far as possible. Suddenly it is warm again; Moser is only about a hundred paces away from me, already on the inner walls, is now walking more slowly. I had wondered at the speed with which Moser trotted across the meadow, for he is said to suffer from heart disease, and as I know for sure, once or twice a year spends several weeks in a sanatorium for cardiac patients in Holzöster, paid for by the District Health Insurance Fund. On the inner walls he trotted even faster than he had on the meadow, which I haven't had mowed for the past eight months. As long as I live, my son writes," the prince said, "I am thinking now of my breakthrough into reality, of my triumph over my theories, as long as I exist this meadow will never be mowed again; as long as I exist nothing profitable or useful will ever again be done on these fields—on mine! on mine! I think. Never again, do you hear, Doctor, never again, never again," the prince said. "From now on the Saurau fields are nothing but useless, unprofitable fields. . . . Moser is typical of the baseness and depravity of the individual human being, my son writes; Moser is typical, he writes, of the baseness and depravity of the state. Moser can be used for proof of anything except the slightest touch of idealism. He embodies the fact, which surely no one can be entirely ignorant of, that man is base and depraved, and that his begetter, insofar as he is the begetter, is even baser and more depraved than he himself. *Moser discredits the world and its creator.* Suddenly I think, my son writes, isn't it wretched to play a part before such a person as Moser? I should have received him right at the door, where I was still preoccupied with the most ludicrous thoughts about Moser. But no, my son writes, I won't receive him at the door. That would only be reacting as if I were ready for the poorhouse. For even without the slightest, strangest secret fear of Moser I should from the first have stayed sitting behind my desk in the office and I should have received Moser where I was before I discovered Moser coming. Imagine, I am not able to cope with Moser, whom I always call an idiot whenever I think of him, although I never say the word aloud. *A Saurau is not able to cope with a Moser!* But there was no longer any means of undoing the situation, and so it no longer mattered where I received the town clerk, at the door or in the office. In any case, I think, the man is one of the sort who without more ado would walk right in through an unlocked door into a house or even into a castle, and then open one door after another, hypocritically asking in each room whether anybody is there. But Moser knows, my son writes, that I spend all the time I am not asleep in the office; how he knows that I don't know, but I know that he knows. In saying the name Moser you are naming a person who knows absolutely everything that is useful to him. And he knows, my son writes, that in order to read—the last time, too, he interrupted me in the middle of my reading: Schumpeter, Rosa Luxemburg, Morus, Clara Zetkin—I stay in the office because of the view, not in the library, whenever I am not asleep. And for him it is important to know that when I am in the office I am not there, as my dead father was, working hard on the estate, except insofar as I plan to destroy it, to destroy the entire estate, do you hear, Doctor, to destroy the

entire estate is not precisely a way of working hard for the
Saurau estate! I spend my time meditating on my revenge
upon my father—possibly not only for an injustice centuries
old, but thousands of years old. In the time remaining to me
I shall still be able to define it exactly. This whole vast ances-
tral agricultural enterprise has more and more come to seem
to me a mistake grown to vast proportions, my son writes. I
read in the office, he writes, and the reading disgusts me too,
but still I read. Reading is still the most bearable of all forms
of disgust. For Moser it is valuable, my son writes, to know
among other things that I stay in the office in order to read.
The fact is that I regard the absurdity of reading among
hundreds of files and calculating machines meant for the
farms and forests, in which nothing is filed and nothing calculated any more—I regard that absurdity *as my father's absurdity*. Here, now that he is dead, I am working out my
revenge complex. Here, where I inhale to the brink of losing
consciousness five hundred years of disciplined labor on
farm and forest, I read Kautsky, Babeuf, Turati, and such
people. My father knows that I have already, although so far
only inside my head, alienated the whole of Hochgobernitz
from its true purposes. And he certainly scents that total
alienation where he is. In heaven? So I sit reading in the
office, my son writes—listen to what he writes, Doctor," the
prince said, "and Moser goes around saying: Young Saurau
now reads in the office where his father worked! Moser often
asks, and always at the moment most favorable to him, my
son writes," the prince said, *"what I am or what I am not,*
but he always says that I am crazy. I hear, even when I do
not hear, how he constantly says I am crazy. Whenever he
speaks of me anywhere the word *damaging* occurs, neither

too frequently nor too rarely, even though whenever *he* says *a spoiled son* it sounds miserable because everything about Moser is miserable. But Moser is careful not to *appear* miserable. I think: Actually and oddly enough, Moser never appears ridiculous to my eyes, my son writes," the prince said, "never, because his baseness is without sharpness, without any comical or tragicomical element. He annoys me and is hated by the few people who have schooled themselves to insight into human nature, but whenever I think of Moser, my son writes, even my annoyance turns into hatred. The defect annoys me, but I hate Moser. Here I am engaged in a task which demands the fullest mental effort, the capacity to exert ever more painful discipline in order to draw everything insofar as it is possible on the thread of a single thought from far below the horizon up out of the void. When such a person as Moser appears, he scatters by his approach all that has been painfully pinned down for use and for consumption. To the degree that Moser approaches, he destroys what I have discovered in the course of reading for a whole morning and half an afternoon, and as soon as Moser is there, nothing at all is left, my son writes. Moser, my son writes; proved this contention by his present approach. I suddenly felt a depressing relaxation of the brain, an increasing sense that I am lost, obviously; because of Moser the intensity is displaced into what is trivial to me. I could say it more simply, my son writes," the prince said. "Moser *comes* and my intelligence *goes*. I was struck by the self-importance with which these base creatures walk, my son writes, for Moser was now no more than a few steps away from me. Every step a Moser takes is taken as if he were important. Stupidity takes these steps, I think. Whereas people of ac-

ceptable intelligence walk casually, often utterly casually, the
base, low person walks self-importantly. The extraordinary
person walks casually, my son writes. But workmen, for example, and farmers, people who work with their hands in
general, walk self-importantly. But I also reckon among the
self-important walkers three quarters of the entire intelligentsia, my son writes. The journalists, the writers, the art-
ists, all bureaucrats, walk self-importantly, and the most self-
important walkers of all are the new politicians. Those who
take the most casual steps of all," the prince said, "those who
walk utterly casually and therefore have the gait of genius,
my son writes, are only the independent in spirit. But when
do we ever see someone who is independent in spirit? Actually my father had, my son writes, not entirely a casual walk,
but still a more casual one, and my grandfather set no store
on his walk at all. . . . Oddly enough, Moser's walk always
reminds me of the walk of many different kinds of convicts
at one and the same time. . . . Moser really has some of the
air of a captured criminal, but in everything about him there
is also something implying a secret that only he knows.
Something triumphant. I have frequently thought about
what the underlying nastiness of Moser is, wherein his baseness lies. The moment he stands before me, I think: He
dares! Without managing to sum up in my mind just what it
is he dares. I say to myself: How dare this man! And he
wants to shake hands with me, but I don't take his hand.
Moser doesn't even expect me to admit him, my son writes; I
have never yet admitted him to Gobernitz. He doesn't know
the castle from inside, not at all, but he would not be Moser,
my son writes," the prince said, "if he were not acquainted
with the interior of the castle in spite of that. There it is

again, the uncanniness that invariably comes at me when
Moser approaches. If Moser so much as entered the vestibule
I would have felt that the place was soiled for a lifetime. The
cunning with which these Mosers lie in wait for some poor
devil and denounce him, the way these Mosers are always
sniffing out circumstantial evidence on everything; these
Mosers bring everybody into court, I think, or at least into
disrepute. Because I did not shake hands with him, my son
writes, and because I gave him no greeting at all, Moser has
taken a step backward. These Mosers are always on the look-
out for something that can involve others in criminality.
What a nose they have for every slightest weakness, what an
instinct for exploiting weaknesses. I think, my son writes:
Imagine masses of Mosers who suddenly emerge from everywhere and begin running things everywhere and finally
dominate everything! I have cheated Moser out of his pref-
ace, my son writes; now he has to come to the point immediately: the harvest! I said I had no time, my son writes; I said
he was disturbing me, that I was working, that I imagine he
is not unaware that I work by reading, that I am working on
Marx's dissertation, on his *Opinions on the Relationship of
the Physics of Democritus and Epicurus,* on *The Difficulties
in Regard to the Identity of the Natural Philosophy of
Democritus and Epicurus.* And I actually said a word to
Moser for the first time, my son writes, the word *reading,* to
indicate that I had no time for his pleadings. I said I wondered that Moser had come, my son writes. After all, he was
aware of my decision to let the harvest rot, aware of my decision to let Hochgobernitz decay, to liquidate Hochgobernitz,
aware of my consistent resolve to destroy Hochgobernitz, my
son writes, Doctor. I said I did not understand his not under-

standing what I am doing, but I know what I am doing, **my** son writes," the prince said. "Nevertheless Moser now proposes to me, for the third time, imagine, my son writes, that I allow some of the townspeople, the majority recruited from the old-age home, into the Hochgobernitz fields, into *my* fields, so that they can harvest the crops! They would like to *harvest* before everything rots! Moser dared to say that already a good deal has rotted and furthermore to ask was I aware of that and, but he did not say this outright, that I am crazy and my father would turn over in his grave on my account, that only a madman did not harvest, only a madman would let such a flourishing farm run down. And actually, my son writes, Doctor, the fact that I am letting my paternal inheritance run down and be destroyed is in truth a monstrous act! Actually I am surely the only person in Central Europe who is letting nine thousand six hundred acres run down! Now for Moser's world, the whole world of the township—the whole ordinary world is a Moser world, the whole state is a Moser state—it is in itself a monstrous act that for a reason they absolutely cannot fathom I have sold all the livestock, have sold off all the movable inventory from the Hochgobernitz fields, have driven all the people out of the house—within one week after the old man's suicide I had them out of the house! Today that seems to me my greatest feat, my son writes," the prince said. "My son writes: It is splendid that I also sent my father's sisters packing, every single one of them! That with one fell swoop I had Hochgobernitz entirely to myself, that is splendid! But then, my son writes, everyone might have thought that I meant to run a completely automated farm, without livestock and without people. . . . But soon they saw that I was not running any

kind of farm at all, that my whole aim was to destroy the
entire business, to destroy all of Hochgobernitz. Within a
single morning I got rid of all the machinery and tractors.
The monstrosity of my act surpassed their strength, and they
informed the courts, the district and state governments. In
vain. . . . All that comes back into my memory now, my
son writes, the very moment that Moser again throws at me
that word *harvest*. You see, Moser says, they'd like to *harvest*
before everything rots. I can't be serious about letting everything rot, he says! But Moser too knows there is no law that
can prescribe what I must do on the combined estates that
make up Hochgobernitz. Harvest! Again I hear what I have
heard often before, about distress in the township, distress of
the people, human distress, poverty, community, *race,* the
problem of vermin, and so on, my son writes. But how does
this man dare, he writes, to repeatedly bring up a subject that
is finished with. *Hochgobernitz is finished!* I am totally
committed to my consistent decisions. I say: *Herr Moser, you
are disturbing me!* my son writes. That is all. I do not have
the strength to turn my back, to ignore Moser. He is here!
Moser is here! For a moment I see all the roads and paths
leading to my fields, which I have blocked off. Everywhere
signs have been posted: *No trespassing.* The town clerk, too,
has to obey that prohibition, for here on my property trespassing is forbidden *to all, to everybody!* Except the deliver-
ers of newspapers. I now see myself once more digging
ditches in the roads, felling tree trunks over them, unrolling
hundreds and hundreds upon hundreds of yards of barbed
wire, my son writes. Doctor," the prince said, "doesn't all
this strike you as *uncanny?* Naturally, my son writes, what I
am doing cannot help seeming insane, but that does not dis-

turb me. The Moser tone has always pained me; these Mosers don't give up, they keep trying again and again, always under some different pretext; but today there is an unbearable stench of insistence about him. He talks about public health! I am abandoning theory for practice, my son writes: But I discover, he writes, no trace of uncertainty in myself. At the moment the uncertainty is all Moser's, and I think: I do not recall ever having greeted Moser, not a single time. And now, listen, Doctor, he writes: My father too never greeted Moser, but that did not prevent the town clerk, whenever I met him or whenever my father met him, every single time, from pushing his way into me or into my father for one painful moment by greeting us. The utter trickery of it! His purpose was to soil one or the other of us. Once the Mosers penetrate into you everything inside you is leprous, my son writes. Such a person can never be *tolerated,* he writes, no, such a person *can* never be tolerated. I hear, my son writes, that he has already recruited the people he needs for harvesting the Hochgobernitz fields, and he says *on behalf of the mayor, of course, and on behalf of public health.* They have all been told to be at the town hall at six tomorrow morning, he says; all they are waiting for is my permission! For permission from above, handed down from Hochgobernitz! I think that people are always obtaining permission from above, always handed down from a Hochgobernitz. But I will permit nothing! The township will supply the implements, the machines, Moser says. It is estimated, Moser says again and again, looking at me and not looking at me, my son writes, that the yield will suffice to feed a few thousand people for a period of more than half a year! No, I say, and Moser says that this year's crop is the best crop. The town clerk is clever at cutting his sentences short because he knows that even his hints are enough to get on my nerves. *Before everything rots,* Moser says emotionally. I hear him speak several times about doing good, but I am deaf to this notion; there is no such thing as doing good, I say. A high hourly wage has been agreed on for harvesting my fields, Moser says, but he does not say how high an hourly wage. No matter what the season, I think, this man always has the same winter woolens on, these cheap, heavy winter wartime woolens that his body slowly fills out, his body which I once saw completely naked, my son writes," the prince said. "I see Moser's flesh more and more growing into those wartime woolens. I once saw him naked by the river, together with his equally naked wife; I remember that infantile penis. There they were, indulging their pitiable Sunday connubiality behind the bushes, away from the clear water, where they thought they were alone and could indulge themselves in their revolting intimacies, succumbing to their stupor in the sunset. The harvesting had to be started at once, Moser said, otherwise *everything* would rot. A short while later I hear the word *inhumanity* repeated. Again and again I hear the word *inhumanity.* Now, at this third attempt to save Hochgobernitz, Moser dares to use that word, and I think: As long as I exist, nothing more will ever be harvested here, on my estates; that is going to be my object for all the future; I am destroying Hochgobernitz. He dares! the masses have become megalomaniac. The word inhumanity, which the masses through Moser have dared to utter here in the courtyard of Hochgobernitz, preoccupies me for some time, time that, failing in my attempt to return to my reading, to return to my science, I fill by reading through

sentences I do not understand. Moser has failed, I say to myself, but I too have failed. Moser is escaping, but I too am
escaping. Where to? Moser's defeat, the defeat of the masses,
is also my own defeat. But my defeat is much more depressing a one than Moser's, I think. Vexation gives way to a
weariness that leads to nothing significant. I look out
through the window, my son writes, and see Moser between
the walls. A short while later I think: Moser walked there,
walked away, I can see where he walked away. *Inhumanity!*
I could no longer bear staying in the castle and put on my
boots and went out of the castle and walked first on the inner
and then on the outer walls, and peered down with my bin-
oculars to determine to what extent everything has already
rotted, my son writes," the prince said. "Isn't it curious," the
prince said, "so long a roll of paper and I see every word of it.
So it is no longer a mystery to me what will happen after my
death," the prince said. "It is all perfectly clear to me."

We were now walking on the outer wall of the castle.
"Down there, do you see," the prince said, "lies Hauenstein.
And there is Stiwoll. And there Köflach. Last night," he said,
"I was down in the gorge. I intended to go into the mill, but
I could not endure the noise the birds in the big cage behind
the mill were making, that horrible screeching. I climbed up
out of the gorge again at once," he said. "Although I am not
alone, I keep entirely to myself. Whereas I myself in the
course of time have almost completely isolated myself from
all society and no longer receive visits," the prince said, "the
women folk hurl themselves more and more into an absolutely bestial form of social absurdity. As you know, I have
even given up playing chess with Krainer. I have discon-
tinued everything that has to do with human associations.

Nowadays I associate only with people with whom I must associate. I maintain only the most minimal kind of business associations. Doesn't the grain interest you, doesn't the whole farm economy interest you any longer? I often ask myself. The foresters, yes, they still interest me, the workmen on the Saurau estates. No one else. It is different for the women. Their Wednesday evenings are unbearable to me. Their Saturday evenings still more unbearable. I refuse to appear at any of these evenings. But I can hear all the way up to my room the way they call out to each other—and they have been doing it this way for decades—the names of those who will be coming up to Hochgobernitz on Wednesday evening or Saturday evening. Miserable people. Most people have gone into liquidation on the day of their birth. Repulsive people from the city, but even more repulsive people from the immediate vicinity, boring, torpid neighbors. By Tuesday they are already moving chairs and benches and tables about the whole house for the Wednesday people, and by Friday for the Saturday people. I hear the clatter of dishes, and I can no longer work, I can no longer think! The clink of silver and of glasses dominates Hochgobernitz, you see. They call me, but I do not answer. They want me, but I will not go down to them. These Wednesday evenings cost a great deal of money, but the Saturday evenings cost even more. On these occasions our graves are opened for hours at a time, their stench released; the huge family graveyards are opened and their peace shattered by talk. The whole countryside is talked to pieces, until everyone is tired and in common disgust trudges out of the castle and back down into the lowlands. On Wednesday and Saturday human vermin dominate here at Gobernitz," the prince said. "Human defectiveness, the onanism of despair," he said. His son could study his future life by the example of his father, he added. The aims for which his father has lived will also be his son's aims, the father's pleasures the son's pleasures, the father's disgust with the world also the son's disgust with the world. After all, the son is going to die after his father, in a loneliness that can be entered and left only within his own brain. When the son looks at his father he sees the father's wretchedness, just as the father constantly sees the son's wretchedness. Father and son continually look at one another in their wretchedness. "But ultimately the son must be much more horrible than the father." He often observed his family from the library window, the prince said, going back and forth in the courtyard in the midst of their conversations. "Locked up in their primitive vocabulary, *radically idle creatures,* my relatives are unthinkable without me," the prince said. This thought would often drive away his boredom in favor of an irrelevant disgust for their bodies. "These bodies that have come from me," he said, "begotten by me without the slightest partiality for life on my part." Suddenly he remarked that at Hochgobernitz derangements often persisted for weeks. "What is the reason?" he asked. "I am not alone in being affected by these derangements," he said. "We are all affected. We all live close together cramped into a building, don't imagine it is big, and are hundreds of thousands of miles apart. We do not hear one another when we call. For weeks at a time we are ruled by the weather, like a catastrophic primal nervous system of which we are merely part. Until we have reached an ultimate degree of depression in which we suddenly begin to talk again, help one another up, begin to understand one another, only to revert once more to our old estrangement. Who is it takes the first step toward intimacy, toward familial attentiveness?" he said. "We eat together again, drink together, talk together, laugh together, until we are separated again. But the time of closeness becomes increasingly shorter." In past years, he said, his son had come back from England to rest up, to show himself, for talk, summertime conversations, and to see the performance of the play—"A three act play is performed at Hochgobernitz every year," the prince said, "with prelude and postlude." But this year his son had been expected not only for pleasure, but chiefly for conversations with his father, "of a legal nature, concerning the property." In letters to his son, which the prince wrote almost daily, he had repeatedly alluded to his plans for Hochgobernitz. He had stressed his resolve to increase the size of the property while at the same time drastically simplifying the methods for its maintenance and administration. "But such fundamental changes cannot be explained in writing," the prince said, "and after all not only Hochgobernitz is involved, but also Ötz and Terlan, the gravel pits near Gmunden, and the town houses in Vienna." But all the while his son had been in Hochgobernitz, the subject had been passed over as quickly as usual, with not a single discussion of these problems. "He thinks he will stay another four or five years in London," the prince said. "I don't know what he intends, I can only guess. This thing he is writing is an altogether political work. Even during the holidays I noticed that he devoted most of his time to this scholarly, actually altogether political work. But he told me that the holidays this year had been *ideal*. Sometimes he too suffers from inability to concentrate," the prince said. "He again made me aware that it is sometimes worthwhile interrupting a prolonged scholarly task that demands the greatest effort to approach an intuitable though unattainable goal. On the Channel boat, he said, he realized that Hochgobernitz is wholly alien to him. I do not believe that is so. My son said he was afraid of Hochgobernitz, in spite of himself. On the one hand it is good to come home for holidays, he said; how easily an intellectual task can go wrong, he said, because one did not dare interrupt it at the decisive moment and at a crucial passage, because one did not obey nature. This decisive moment came for him, my son, shortly before the holidays. It had been right, he said, to interrupt the work at the moment that I wrote to him: Come here! But I wanted to have him in Hochgobernitz, with me, for a particular end. I did not attain this end. But the usefulness of his interrupting his work satisfied him," the prince said. "I saw clearly, while my son was on his way from England and drawing nearer to Hochgobernitz, the rough spots, the deterioration in the relationship between us. They increased from hour to hour. Then my son arrived and I saw these faults distinctly. He said he was working on an essay he had been able to rescue. He lives in a perpetually sunless little room, bare and cheap, though in the vicinity of Hyde Park. My son has to exhaust himself," the prince said. "Once he has utterly exhausted himself, he comes back."

The prince said: "The last time my son was here I persuaded him to take a walk down into the gorge. At supper he agreed that we would take a walk down into the gorge early in the morning. And in fact we did rise early and go down into the gorge. This walk," the prince said, "was once again one of those walks I love, *without a word spoken*. It goes without saying, Doctor, that on such walks there must not be a word spoken. Anyone who does not abide by this rule will never share such a walk with me again. But on this morning, with the landscape suddenly darkening because of course we were descending into the gorge, even though the day was brightening, on this morning I myself suddenly began speaking. I said to my son that for some time I have had a pain in my head, that these noises are in my head, and I said that this pain and these noises were becoming more and more unbearable. These noises, I said, have made it impossible for me to think out anything, no matter what. And yet, I said to my son, it is tremendously important right now to think out the matter that at the moment occupies my thoughts, Hochgobernitz. These noises, I said, shatter everything for me. Pain and noises are the same thing, I said. Possibly, I said to my son as we reached the bottom of the gorge, these noises and this pain are no more nor less than my fatal illness. *Possibly.* I said: I am fatally ill, my dear boy. And I said: Isn't that sad, my dear boy? But he said nothing. Whenever I look at people, I look at unhappy people," the prince said. "They are people who carry their torment into the streets and thus make the world a comedy, which is of course laughable. In this comedy they all suffer from tumors both mental and physical; they take *pleasure* in their fatal illness. When they hear its name, no matter whether the scene is London, Brussels, or Styria, they are frightened, but they try not to show their fright. All these people conceal the actual play within the comedy that this world is. Whenever they feel themselves unobserved, they run away from themselves toward themselves. Grotesque. But we do not even see the most ridiculous side of it because the most ridiculous side is always the reverse side. God sometimes speaks to them, but he uses the same vulgar words as they themselves, the same clumsy phrases. Whether a person has a gigantic factory or a gigantic farm or an equally gigantic sentence of Pascal's in his head, is all the same," the prince said. "It is poverty that makes people the same; at the human core, even the greatest wealth is poverty. In men's minds and bodies poverty is always simultaneously a poverty of the body and a poverty of the mind, which necessarily makes them sick and drives them mad. Listen to me, Doctor, all my life I have seen nothing but sick people and madmen. Wherever I look, the worn and the dying look back at me. All the billions of the human race spread over the five continents are nothing but one vast community of the dying. Comedy!" the prince said. "Every person I see and everyone I hear anything about, no matter what it is, prove to me the absolute obtuseness of this whole human race and that this whole human race and all of nature are a fraud. Comedy. The world actually is, as has so often been said, a stage on which roles are forever being rehearsed. Wherever we look it is a perpetual learning to speak and learning to walk and learning to think and learning by heart, learning to cheat, learning to die, learning to be dead. This is what takes up all our time. Men are nothing but actors putting on a show all too familiar to us. Learners of roles," the prince said. "Each of us is forever learning one (his) or several or all imaginable roles, without knowing why he is learning them (or for whom). This stage is an unending torment and no one feels that the events on it are a pleasure. But everything that happens on this stage happens naturally. A critic to explain the play is constantly being sought. When the curtain rises, everything is over." Life, he went on, changing his image, was a school in which death was being taught. It was filled with millions and billions of pupils and teachers. The world was the school of death. "First the world is the elementary school of death, then the secondary school of death, then, for the very few, the university of death," the prince said. People alternate as teachers or pupils in these schools. "The only attainable goal of study is death," he said. His son had told him that in London he sometimes woke up and dressed and tore out of the house and down Oxford Street imagining that at the end of Oxford Street there would be the Ache, from which Hochgobernitz can be seen. "All people are more or less crazy, of course, even my son," the prince said. Actually, he went on, his son's madness must be extraordinary "if it is true that he tears down Oxford Street believing he'll find the Ache at its end. If you wish, you can look into the Ache always and everywhere," the prince said. "Every man has his own Ache, every man has a different Ache. I myself," he said, "often wake up and dress and go down into the yard and out through the gate to the inner or the outer wall, and am in reality going through Brussels." Inside every human head is the human catastrophe corresponding to this particular head, the prince said. It is not necessary to open up men's heads in order to know that there is nothing inside them but a human catastrophe. "Without his human catastrophe, man does not exist at all," the prince said. Man loves his misery, he said, and if he is without his misery for a moment, he does everything he can to return into his misery. "When we look at people, they are either in their misery or seeking their misery. There are no individuals who are free of human misery," he said. Man exists continually in an extremely dangerous state, the prince said, but he is not conscious of the fact that he continually exists in an extremely dangerous state, forever opposed to himself. This is the basis of his existence, but this is also the basis of his sickness. "All dying," the prince said. "Probably children are begotten by their parents out of sheer malice and dragged into the world out of the greatest imaginable inconsiderateness. When we seek a person," the prince said, "it is as if we go about in a vast morgue looking for him." All the things that people say are said only in monologues, the prince said. "We are in an age of monologues. The art of the monologue is also a far higher art than the art of dialogue," he said. "But monologues are just as pointless as dialogues, although in a way much less pointless. Whenever you engage in a dialogue with another person (with yourself!) because otherwise you are suddenly afraid of suffocating, you must be prepared for his doing his utmost to undercut you. That can be done in the subtlest, the most elaborate, but also the nastiest manner. Whenever people talk they undercut one another. The art of conversation is an art of undercutting, and the art of monologue is the most horrible kind of undercutting. I always think," the prince said, "that my interlocutor is trying to push me down into his own abyss after I have just barely managed to escape from my own abyss. Your interlocutors try to push you into as many abysses as possible simultaneously. All interlocutors are always mutually pushing one another into all abysses." The prince went on to say that he often went to bed with a particular classical melody, or a still irregular one, in his head, and woke up with the same melody there. "Must I assume," the prince said, "that this melody remained in my head all night long? Of course. As you know, I always tell myself, everything is always in your head. Everything is always in all heads. Only in all heads. There is nothing outside of heads. No matter what I am talking about with whom," the prince said, "by the very act of talking with someone I am finished. A grown-up person is in principle infinite; one not yet grown up is infinite like nature." The majority of mankind devotes itself wholly to its two chief pursuits, purchasing and consuming, he said. "Strictly speaking, over the course of millennia, as we now see," the prince said, "men have developed only these two instincts, the instinct to buy and the instinct to consume. Perhaps that shocks us," Prince Saurau said, "perhaps we should be horrified by this." Everyone, he went on, speaks a language he does not understand, but which *now and then* is understood by others. That is enough to permit one to exist and at least to be misunderstood. If there were language that could be understood, nothing more would be needed. "We have always found refuge in a problem," he said. "People walk with one another and talk with one another and sleep with one another and do not know one another. If people knew one another they would not walk, talk, or sleep with one another. Do you know yourself? I often ask myself," Prince Saurau said. A depth is always a height, the deeper the depth of the height, the higher the height of the depth, and vice versa, he added. "You imagine," the prince said, "that you peer down into an infinite well (as into an infinite person), into his infinite height, size, and so on. . . . I *believe* that my son is in London because I *know* that he is in London; I *believe* I am writing him a letter because I *know* I am writing him a letter, but I do not *know* that he is in London because I *believe* that he is in London, and so on. . . . Impossibility is a ghastly foundation," he said. "Everything is based on impossibility. I called my elder sister. I asked her to walk down to the river with me and she walked down to the river with me. But as we returned I thought: Has she really been by the river with me? I am in a continual state of torment, Doctor. Aren't all these things signs of a brutal realization of death in me? I never think of my wife any longer," the prince said, although of all people she was the one he had loved most. He also wondered why he no longer dreamed of her. "For years I have not dreamed of my wife," he said. "I neither think of her nor dream of her. She is *gone*. Gone where? Of course she still exists, because I am now speaking of her. You know, Doctor, the tragedy is that nothing is ever really dead. About my son: I want to meet him at the station. I write that to him, and he replies that he does not want to be met. He *suddenly* comes in at the door. His actions have always been completely unpredictable. We always shared a fondness for reading newspapers. Even in its initial stages a personality like my son's is complete. I don't like expressions such as *sense perception* and so on, which my son uses so often. Moreover, I, in contrast to him, am totally opposed to quotations. Quoting gets on my nerves. But we are sequestered in a world that is constantly quoting, in a constant quotation that *is* the world, Doctor. And what do you think of a sentence like: *But chance, not God, as the common herd believes, must be assumed.* My son deals in such sentences. All actions are punishable actions and that is why it is so easy to straightway make a punishable action out of any action. That is why it is possible to pronounce and to carry out justified sentences of death upon everyone. The state has recognized this fact. The state is founded on it. I still employ words that my son finds unendurable, such as *melancholia, loyal, tremendous, pain-*

*ful, fatal*. My pantheism, his apostasy," the prince said. "My son has actually succumbed to a sham metaphysics. We are, to be sure, neutral apparatuses driven by a tremendous galvanism. The aimlessness in which we more and more lose our sense of direction has been constantly in my thoughts of late, catastrophically concrete. My son," the prince said, "used to dress very elegantly. Now he doesn't care what he has on. He has donned the proletariat, and the horrible part of it is that at any moment he can strip himself of it again. That is what is terrifying. In the past he swiftly arrived at good opinions; now he slowly comes to wrongheaded ones. Our distance apart increases, and the tension between us likewise. The world as a whole has already become entirely provincial. For a long time Nature permitted him, my son, to develop quite unobtrusively among his sisters. But all of a sudden this same Nature in the most amazing manner cruelly developed his intellectual endowments as if they were exclusively directed against those sisters still drifting in the daze of childhood and youth. He has always been a problem in the sense of being continually disjunct from us. We, his parents, bent all our efforts to leading him ever closer to the boundaries of truth. Even though we ourselves could not perceive the truth, we nevertheless knew, his mother and I, where its boundaries are. Whenever he was in cities he always reported that he was happy, but about his stays in the country the word was always *unhappy, unhappy*. Later, during his university studies, he always left us unexpectedly; he even got up and went out of our thoughts without excuse. Between the ages of twenty-one and twenty-three he would shut himself up in his room for days, not even leaving it for meals, for the sake of his thoughts. Each of us has protracted periods in which we do not exist at all, only pretend to exist. Sometimes the actual existence and the pretended existence of a person merge in a way that is fatal for him. Everything in Hochgobernitz is focused on my son, but my son is only dominated by Hochgobernitz; he does not focus on it. Sometimes he unexpectedly has knowledge of things that astonish me, though what he knows has *absolutely no application* to anything. When he comes home and assumes his inheritance, everything will rot. He started going to school at the age of four and a half, feeling it to be a means for *relaxing* his mind. We always associate him with accidents. Whenever someone has tumbled into the gorge, we think it must be our son. An entirely ontological type," the prince said. "His last visit was one unbroken period of gloom lasting over four weeks and spreading through all of us. All Hochgobernitz was under a pall of gloom. Even while he was still in England my son cast this pall over Hochgobernitz weeks before he arrived home, and then when he did come to Hochgobernitz he cast that pall of gloom over all of us. The nervous states of the women often permeate the entire landscape too. In the lower rooms, the women's rooms, there is order, in the upper rooms, mine, disorder. But the order is where the disorder is. Strictly speaking," the prince said, "the methods my son uses to distance himself from me are really my own. There are people who manage quite well with the raw materials of life and do not refine it; the raw materials suffice them. Everything in my son's letters, except for himself, is mere backdrop; ideas are nothing but sets dropped from the grid of the universe, and his brain is nothing but a highly complicated modern stage-lighting system which constantly influences these sets. I am constantly looking through this

political theater life he leads, at his horrible financial predic-
ament. Madness is more bearable and the world at bottom is
a carnival. For the women time drags more and more, for
me the more it drags the less it drags. Absolute ataraxy, that
is my state. Suicide," the prince said, "a climacterium. We
have the highest suicide rate in Europe. Why? Now, in the
middle of the century, we have not been able to elaborate any
other theme but that of suicide. Everything is suicide. Whatever we live, whatever we read, whatever we think—all
manuals for suicide. The dead," the prince said, "are more
attractive than those who haven't yet reached that stage. No
matter what we are reminded of, what our attention is called
to, we are reminded of death, our attention is called to death.
Standing at the window in the night, watching several acro-
bats walking tightropes stretched across infinity—to call out
to them is to incur the death penalty. But whenever we speak
of suicide there is something *comical* about it. *I put a bullet
into (or through) my head, I shoot, I hang myself*—all are
comical. How can I ask you to trust me, I wrote to my son
yesterday, when I do not trust you on a single point? I do not
trust my son on a single point. It is true you have spent your
money, but you have yet to prove to me that you have in-
vested it well in your brain as one invests it well in a bank or
in the stock market. I have always had my doubts about the
brain as a stock market or bank. Of course you can also regard your brain as a power plant which delivers current to
the whole world. . . . Do you know," the prince said, "my
son has had his eye on nothing but my fortune. I don't believe in those studies of his. In London he is throwing
himself away on a piece of sham. Losing his head over world
history. A regrettable enthusiasm. What irritates me is that I

do not see my son spending much of his time in good restaurants in Haymarket, but always sitting over his essay in his scholar's den. Incidentally," the prince said, "the art of listening is nearly extinct. But I observe that you, Doctor, are still practicing it."

Turning to me the prince said that my father should some day take me along on one of the Saurau hunts, which he held two or three times a year. "The Saurau hunts are famous. I personally am no longer interested in them, but to my family they are supremely necessary. We are continually trying out on others what we do not try out on ourselves," the prince said. "We repeatedly kill people and observe this process and its result. Man constantly practices horror upon others, least of all on (or in) himself. We always try out all possible diseases on others; we continually kill others for purposes of study. This morning," the prince said, "I suddenly felt the need to lie flat on the floor, stark naked. I undressed and lay down stark naked on the floor. At breakfast I told the others about it, but nobody laughed." All his life, he said, his thoughts and actions had sprung from his estates, had grown out of Hochgobernitz. "Even what seems utterly remote has come out of my estates, out of Hochgobernitz," he said. "The horizon is the handiest kind of nonsense. This morning," he said, "I made an unusual remark to my elder sister. I said to her: *The poetic is suspect to me because in the world it arouses the impression that the poetic is poetry, and vice versa, that poetry is the poetic. The only poetry, I said, is nature, the only nature is poetry. The only consistent concept, Doctor.*"

Suddenly, that morning, he had felt the need to read aloud to the women a section from Goethe's *The Elective*

*Affinities.* But when they were all assembled in the library, he suddenly had the feeling that it was pointless to read to them from *The Elective Affinities,* and instead he had read to them from an old *Times.* "I wanted to read to the women the chapter beginning *The scaffolding stood ready . . . ,*" he said, "and instead I read to them how potatoes are stored for the winter in England. As soon as I had finished reading them how potatoes are stored in England, I bowed them out of the library and called: To work! To work! To work, idiots! Shortly afterward I went down into the yard and read the chapter *The scaffolding stood ready . . .* to myself. Undisturbed. Untainted. Unfeminized!

"I very often see my son somewhere on a London street that I am familiar with from my own days of studying in London. Trees. People. People as trees. Trees as people. My son is wearing the same suit I wore when I was in London. Sometimes he walks across Trafalgar Square or through Hyde Park with *my* thoughts. With *my* problems. And I think: He is crossing Trafalgar Square and walking through Hyde Park with your problems. My son sits with my thoughts on the very bench in Hyde Park where I sat. And he thinks, while he is sitting on my Hyde Park bench, of Hochgobernitz, just as I thought of Hochgobernitz when I was there. When you think of Hochgobernitz while you are in London," the prince said, "you imagine that Hochgobernitz is an entirely unchanged Hochgobernitz, just as in Hochgobernitz when you think of London you think that London has not changed, has remained unchanged although Hochgobernitz at every moment is a completely changed Hochgobernitz. And I think: He is sitting on the Hyde Park bench or walking through the Tate Gallery and thinking about me, because when I was in London going through the Tate Gallery to see the Blakes, I thought of my father. I think: My son in London thinks of his father in Hochgobernitz just as the father thinks of his son in London. Constantly seeing Hochgobernitz in London makes you as sick and demented, I imagine, as constantly seeing London in Hochgobernitz. And I see and *hear* London," the prince said, "just as my son in London sees *and* hears Hochgobernitz. But it is always a different London and always a different Hochgobernitz."

Only in London, the prince said, did his son think his mind could develop in all directions, but he, his son's father, was convinced that his son's mind could develop in all directions only in Hochgobernitz. "Of course," the prince said, "the mind is not limited by being in London. But it is also not limited by being in Hochgobernitz."

The last time my father had visited him, the prince had kept repeating the phrase "tangle of lines," the prince recalled. Everything had been appearing to him as a "tangle of lines." He had said to my father then: "There is a tangle of lines in my head." Once, when the two of them, after the steward's death, had called on the tenant farmers, he had repeatedly remarked that the tenants were "corporeals" with whom he had to "settle accounts." One had to settle accounts with the corporeals, he had said several times, and likewise: "One had to settle accounts with corporeality. Everything is a matter of settling with corporeality." He was rapidly wearing himself out in frightful privations, he now said. He had been born into Hochgobernitz as into a vacuum, by an *unsuspecting mother*. And he was always speaking in words that really no longer existed. "The words we speak really no longer exist," the prince said. "The whole instrumentation of words that we use no longer exists. Still it is not possible to fall utterly silent. No," he said. "The employment of life as a science, a science of political administration," he said. "Among the special abilities I was early able to observe in myself," he said, "is the ruthlessness to lead anyone I choose through his own brain until he is nauseated by this cerebral mechanism. For it's fatal in any case, Doctor, in any case. My son blames me for my age," he said, "and I him for his youth. My age is in itself naïve, but my son's youth is not in itself naïve."

The prince said he was forever compelled to make a stupid society realize it was stupid, and that he was always doing everything in his power to prove to this stupid society how stupid it was. But sometimes this stupid society would say that *he* was stupid. "That's their only way out," he said. "Of course, for a long period in my life I always had a friend, but my son has not had that. Why? The science on which he is engaged excludes a friend. This science destroys everything, *everything* there is, Doctor. One of these days this science will have destroyed everything. And because this science must destroy everything, it is naïve. We deal only with naïve sciences. For me it has never been difficult to share my brain with others at times, but my son can never share his brain with anyone else.

"The modernity *in* a brain refreshes me," he said, *"the inner modernity*. The other modernity repels me. The modernity we don't see refreshes me," he said, "the invisible sort that propels everything onward, not the visible kind that propels nothing." Last night, he said, he had got up and gone down into the library and had said to the books: *My food!* "But now this food is all poisoned," he said. "Deadly."

At the moment he decided to lead us from the inner wall back to the outer wall again, he noted "a very painful continuity of the noises" inside his brain. "Sometimes I am delighted by the fact that I am left entirely to myself and am full of pain." He often worried, he said, over the thought of his death not being discovered for a long time by the people around him. "Everything I am telling you," he said, "is largely esoteric. I have never seen my son laughing. Nor his mother—Doctor, did you ever see your mother laughing? No, you never saw her laughing. And has your son seen his mother laughing? No, he never saw her laughing. But I myself often used to have reason to laugh, in the past. Now I often laugh without any reason, you see. I became aware of my son's dislike for fairy tales when he was quite young. And on the other hand his sister's frightening partiality for fairy tales. He attributes too much to me. Everybody attributes too much to me. The chaos is already so great that everyone attributes much too much. But whereas his sisters always express their opinions about a thing prematurely, he does not express his opinions prematurely. But, Doctor, I am speaking about myself only in quotation marks, as you know; everything I say is said only in quotation marks. Murmured! Every day I wake up and think: To whom am I going to bequeath everything? Since nobody else is even possible, I come back to the fact that I must bequeath everything to my only son. But when my son keeps silent, I continually have the feeling that I must defend myself. . . . In the presence of my son all those traits of mine that are repugnant to him (and to me also) come to light. These unbearable traits come to light only in my son's presence, whereas in the pres-

ence of other people still other . . . and so on. I ask myself:
Does my son also have unbearable traits only in my presence? Nowadays we can analyze everything, Doctor, everything but nature. Everything is always a question of the
*nous*. People," the prince said, "early slip into a business as
into a warming suit which they then have on all their lives
until nothing but a tattered rag is left of it. They patch away
at the tattered suit for decades, lining it, widening it, narrow-
ing it, voluntarily or out of coercion, but it always remains
the same tattered rag. You see whole nations running around
in ridiculous, completely tattered rags. All Europe is running
around in completely tattered rags. Everybody slips into a
business as into a suit, and to slip into a course of study is
exactly the same as slipping into a business or a suit. The
majority of those who have slipped into the realm of the
mind have on, in the final analysis, nothing but ridiculous
rags. All of us have on nothing but ridiculous rags. Yesterday I had the notion—I was on my way to breakfast—that I
had ordered all the trees cut down. I look down from the
castle and see nothing but millions of felled trees. Then I
have the idea, how would it be if I first had these millions of
cut trees cut up into pieces three feet long, then into pieces an
inch long, and finally if I had the workmen pulverize them!
Suddenly I saw the whole countryside covered with the sawdust from my trees, and I waded through this sawdust down
to the Mur and then down to the Plattensee. There were no
people to be seen, none left. Probably, I thought, they all
were smothered under the sudden rain of sawdust. Yesterday," the prince said, "the memoirs of Cardinal Retz, which
I have been studying for so long and which have constantly
seemed to me worthwhile studying, suddenly began to irritate

me. How? you will ask. I had been unable to fall asleep because of Cardinal Retz's memoirs. For hours I looked at Cardinal Retz's memoirs and could not fall asleep. But I was incapable of getting up and throwing the book out the window. Finally I did get up and threw Cardinal Retz's memoirs out of the window and realized that I had been looking at them for five hours and that they had been irritating me for five hours without my throwing them out of the window. There are people," he said, "who die with the greatest decisiveness and are decisively dead once and for all. I too would like to die like that. But most people die vaguely, vaguely to the eye and vaguely to the brain. They are never dead. No matter what we amuse ourselves with, we are always preoccupied only with death," he said. "That is essentially human," he said, "that everything takes place in death." Then he said: "My sisters, but my daughters also, try to keep me going by means of little or big deceptions, and by one outrageous deception above all: *their attentiveness*. Each of them knows in her heart," he said, "that the world will collapse when I suddenly am no longer here. When I lose all desire to go on and have myself laid out in the pavilion, I shall have myself laid out in the pavilion like my father. A dead father," he said, "actually inspires fear. For many hours at a time I often think of nothing but the letter carrier. Mail must be coming, I think. Mail! Mail! Mail! News! Some day a message must come that won't disappoint me. From whom? Wouldn't it be delightful, Doctor, to open a letter and say to yourself: Aha, on the twenty-fourth I'll be dead? Suddenly comes the notion that the surface of the earth is gradually turning into completely airless space. I observe people who at first do not know what is happening and stand still in the middle of the street, as is only natural, just as others, as is only natural, walk on, walk faster, walk slower, walk, walk, walk; they go into shops or come out of shops, and suddenly all of them discover this process whose meaning they don't know; they don't know what it is, and one after the other, the weaker first, the stronger next, they fall to the ground. Soon the whole street, all the streets, are littered with suffocated people, corpses; everything has come to a standstill; many disasters caused by unmanned machines are no longer perceived because they have taken place after the complete extinction of mankind and consequently are not disasters at all. . . . The end is a tremendous din followed by a natural process of decay.

"In conversation," the prince said, "people constantly feel as if they are treading a tightrope and are always afraid of falling down to the low level more proper to them. I too have this fear. Therefore all conversations are conducted by people who are treading a tightrope and constantly in fear of falling to their low level, of being pushed down to the low level. In the nature of things it sounds completely different," Prince Saurau said, "when my son in England, in London, says at Victoria Station, for example, that he hates people, completely different from the way it sounds when I in Hochgobernitz say that I hate people, yet it is the same ridiculous hatred for the same ridiculous people. If in Victoria Station we call our mother or our father, it is the same as when we call our mother, our father, from here in Hochgobernitz. Do you see? If we walk consistently, and especially in books, we are in reality always walking through landscapes we have long known. We come upon nothing new. Just as we come upon nothing new in the sciences. Everything is prescribed.

The cold is inside me," the prince said. "Therefore it makes no difference where I go; the cold goes along with me inside me. I am freezing from within. But in the library this cold is most bearable. Nothing but brains printed to death," the prince said. "With every book we discover to our horror a human being printed to death by the printers, a man published to death by the publishers, read to death by the readers. Let's say there's a letter from a wool trader in Bombay to my younger sister, from a friend of her youth. The letter is lying in my sister's desk. I know that. Nevertheless I ask my sister, after I have known for weeks that the letter is lying in her desk: *Where in the world is that letter from Bombay?* And she says, although she knows that I know that the letter is in her desk: *In the desk.* The absurdity in which people get up and in which they go to bed again," he said, "always of course merits another sense of shock. Why not? After all there is always a different absurdity in their getting up and their going to bed. The absurdity in which we are now walking on the wall, for example—are you aware of this absurdity? And is your son aware of it? We face questions like an open grave about to be filled. It is also absurd, you know, for me to be talking of the absurdity," he said. "My character can justly be called thoroughly unloving. But with equal justice I call the world utterly unloving. Love is an absurdity for which there is no place in nature.

"In the course of the changes I intend to make in Hochgobernitz," he said, "everything here is going to be restricted. Everything will be enlarged and everything will be restricted. An enlargement of the estates involves a restriction of our lives. Again and again I reflect that I have been left alone. And I feel this to be the most loathsome of thoughts:

to be left alone. Loneliness is man's route to loathsomeness. Age is an enormous loathsomeness. Youth is disgusting, but age is loathsome. My relatives go back and forth like the dead. Sometimes I have the impulse to summon them and shout into their faces that they ought to stop being permanently dead. It is the same every day," the prince said. "It is cold in my room because it is cold in me; it is cold in Hochgobernitz because it is cold in me. I leave my room, I leave Hochgobernitz—in my thoughts, you understand—and everywhere I feel the same cold. I often think that it is my duty to write to my son in London and tell him what is awaiting him here in Hochgobernitz some day, when I am dead: cold. Isolation. Madness. Deadly monologuing. Madness emerging from himself and appearing as madness of the world, of nature. My father," the prince said, "often spoke of selling Hochgobernitz and everything that belonged to it. At first he wanted to part with the gravel pits, then with the sawmills, then with the mills, then with Hochgobernitz itself, and he ordered his steward, a man named Gombrowicz, to work out a plan for liquidating the entire estate. For days he talked about freeing himself from Hochgobernitz, but when he thought of the workmen, of the gravel pit workmen, of the millers, of the sawyers, who were dependent on Hochgobernitz and therefore upon him alone, he threw up the plan again. . . . Toward the end he frequently said: I am tired, I am tired of Hochgobernitz, but I am too tired to give up Hochgobernitz, I would rather give myself up. It occurs to me," the prince said, "that he imagined a marital union between the steward and my elder sister; he regarded such a union as a future fact. He disliked the steward's looks, and his mind as well, but he *saw* this union and wanted to bring it about. We owe everything to the steward, he always used to say. Then the steward plunged into the gorge and was buried, and another came. Toward the end," the prince said, "my father more and more feared he would have to liquidate Hochgobernitz. But at the end he didn't care about anything. He had a miserable end. His only contact with the women was when he was hungry; with me, to berate me, to curse me. He pushed a note under his door on which was written in red pencil what he wanted to eat or drink." During the last two weeks these notes called only for bread and water, the prince said. He no longer opened the door. He no longer washed either, and sometimes in the early morning they heard him pacing in his room and talking loudly to himself, but they could not make out a word. Suddenly, two days before his suicide, he ceased his incomprehensible monologue. There was complete silence in his room. But it no longer disturbed them, because they had already been rendered completely apathetic. For two weeks old Saurau opened the windows of his room only to pour his excretions, which he took care of in a bucket, out of the window into the courtyard. Before he finally withdrew to his room his family had occasionally seen him sitting at his desk in the office, motionless. He had often left his room in the depths of the night and gone down to the office to seat himself at his desk. His son, who went to him in the office, asked whether he could help him, but his father remained silent. It seemed to the son again and again that the father had something important to say, but could no longer say it. For hours old Saurau would sit in increasing fixity, only to stand up suddenly and return to his room. "The moment my father was in his room," the prince said, "he locked the door." The prince suspected that his father, locked in his room, wept. During the last days the women had been totally unable to do anything with him or for him. "Almost all the Sauraus have killed themselves," the prince said. "Hochgobernitz has ended with suicide for almost all Sauraus." The women had left everything to him, the madman's son. He had had to bear the whole burden, he said. The prince described his father's last day as follows: Until three o'clock in the afternoon he had heard nothing at all from his father's room. He became suspicious about the quiet on his father's floor. In the office he had negotiated with the gravel pit workers, with the sawyers, and then with the forestry apprentices, and during these negotiations he had kept thinking that it was not normal for it to be so quiet at this time. For previously he had always heard his father at least moving back and forth, "*creeping* back and forth," the prince said, "but on that day, the last day of October 1948, I heard nothing." After the gravel pit workers, the sawyers, and the forestry apprentices were gone, he had studied and arranged the papers that had arrived from the county commissioner's office, "including those concerning the flood," the prince said, and then gone into the kitchen and told the women that he would look in on his father. Upstairs, he had knocked on the door repeatedly, but nothing stirred inside the room. "Father!" Nothing. Usually his father had always replied, "though confusedly." Nothing. The son then forced his way into his father's room; he broke open the door with his shoulder. He found his father on the floor in the center of the room with a bullet hole in his head. On the dead man's wrists he had noticed swellings, and immediately connected them with his father's madness. When the district doctor (my father's

predecessor) arrived, the prince had called his attention to
these swellings, but the doctor denied any connection between the swellings and the madness of the prince's father.
"But I still believe, and more strongly than ever, Doctor," the
prince said, "that there was a connection between my father's
insanity and his swollen wrists. I must add, though," the
prince said, "that I have never believed in doctors and that to
this day I don't believe in medical art. You are not here to see
me as a doctor, you know, not as a doctor," the prince said,
"and to this day I believe that doctors are of all people those
farthest removed from human nature, who know least about
human nature." He could imagine, he said, that on the last
day his father had been unable to get up and had only
crawled around in his room. Quite aside from his madness,
the weeks of strictly refusing nourishment had made him
incapable of standing erect. "Toward the end he had no
strength at all left, Doctor," the prince said, "no strength at
all." It had not been hard, the prince had said at the time, to
imagine, as he looked at his father laid out in the pavilion, all
that his father had endured "in order to have the privilege of
being dead at last. All over his body we discovered traces of
cruel torments he had inflicted on himself," the prince said.
His whole body had been marked by self-inflicted bruises.
"This highly intelligent person!" the prince said. "The crucial pages were ripped out of his favorite books, which he
had taken from the library to his room. Pages from *The
World As Will and Idea,* for instance. He had *eaten* them,"
the prince said. "Schopenhauer has always been the best
nourishment for me," his father had written a few hours before his suicide, on a scrap of paper found by a member of
the coroner's commission. It was dated October 22, 1948. He

had torn open his jacket, cut it into narrow longitudinal strips, and twisted these into a rope. "At first he had intended to hang himself," the prince said, "but at the last moment shooting seemed to him better. And so the last communication from him, written on a blank page torn from the front of *The World As Will and Idea,* consisted of the two words *shooting better."* All the circumstances indicated that his father had shot himself hours before the prince found him, "while we were down at the river looking at the receding flood," the prince said. Instinctively, the prince had opened the window of his father's room and for a moment considered whether it might not have been an accident. "But it was certainly suicide," the prince said. "My father shot himself with full deliberation. His madness did not exclude a deliberate intention to kill himself." Even before he informed the women, the prince had telephoned the district doctor. "The fact that he refused to associate the swellings on my father's wrists with his mental illness is a prime example of the ignorance, the narrowmindedness, of doctors," the prince said. The women had stood in his father's room, incapable of doing anything sensible, as if his father had killed them along with himself. A coroner's commission had arrived by half past four—"young fellows," the prince said, "who persistently talked about other incidents which had no bearing on our present concern. The women," the prince said, "carried the body into the bathroom to wash it. Under the direction of the district doctor they tried to hold the shattered skull together with clothespins. They stuffed the bullet hole with cotton dipped in wax. Meanwhile a few workmen were clearing out the pavilion, so that we could lay Father out in there. Because of the play that had been given there a few weeks before, inside the pavilion and not in the yard because of bad weather, the pavilion was still full of dozens of sets, props, costumes, and chairs." He had been surprised at the speed with which the workmen transformed the pavilion into a mortuary hall, the prince commented. As the women carried the body across the yard to the pavilion, they let it drop, so the son had carried his dead father into the pavilion all alone. They merely wrapped him in sheets and covered him with sheets. For several hours blood had continued to flow from his head, and from his mouth and ears, which necessitated frequent changing of the sheets. His father's body was already cold by the time the prince drove down into the town to make arrangements for the funeral. The women passed on the news to the rest of the family. "They have a fantastic routine for funerals," the prince said. "As the cause of death they alleged sudden madness. *Sudden* madness?" the prince said. "The forestry apprentices, the sawyers, and the gravel pit workers were the first aside from our closest relatives to pay their respects to Father in the pavilion," he said. "None of them understood him." After the funeral the weeks rushed by, he said. The affairs of the property had devolved upon him so quickly that it had been at once painful and easy for him. "I am alone," the prince said. And he said: "I cannot take you into the house because everything is in disorder, everything is in disorder." He repeated, "I am alone," while we were caught by the sudden darkness on the inner wall of the castle, "but that doesn't bother anyone. In my solitude I am the most undemanding person of them all. I put on my old suits; in ten years I have not bought a new pair of shoes! I do without everything. Last night," he said, "when my elder daughter returned from an outing to Hohenwart, where she met her lover, I realized fully just how undemanding I am. You're not really here any more, I thought, now *they* are here! As she told me about the visit, I thought that I have departed from my relatives, have come so far from them although I don't know where I am headed, am moving away from them with such speed that I can never return to them. Hochgobernitz is also inside an ever-deepening pall," he said. "Possibly the point in time at which it will be completely overcast is no longer far off. My sisters are talking with a dead man when they talk with me, I think. For my sisters I am only alive theoretically," he said. "But I too have the feeling of talking only with the dead whenever I talk with anyone in the house in that whisper which has for years been the prevailing tone of voice here. The dead awaken and wash themselves and breakfast and talk and separate and crawl back into their beds," Prince Saurau said. "A dead family," he said. "When someone close to us has committed suicide," the prince said, "we ask: Why suicide? We search for reasons, causes, and so on. . . . We follow the course of the life he has now so suddenly terminated as far back as we can. For days we are preoccupied with the question: Why suicide? We recollect details. And yet we must say that everything in the suicide's life—for now we know that all his life he was a suicide, led a suicide's existence—is part of the cause, the reason, for his suicide. The act of suicide always strikes us as sudden. Why? Why, we wonder, were we surprised for so much as a single moment at his suicide? Laid out in the pavilion," the prince said, "my father gave the impression of a man frightened to death. At night his shattered head often appears to me in the strangest contexts. His hands, which the women had folded over the sheets, upset me. I often think of him now. But most of the time I do not see him living, but dead. It is extremely difficult for me to picture my father living. My relationship to him was complicated; but we did not use it against one another," the prince said. "On the walls of the castle I can endure my solitude because I am completely alone on the walls. Have I always been alone? You should be able to say something about that, Doctor," the prince said. "You are not alone, after all. Perhaps I ought to put it: You are not yet alone. Or: The father is always farther along than the son, and vice versa, the son always farther along than the father, and so on. . . . Yes," he said, "sometimes I recall the scene I once saw in Brussels: A man is walking and looking into shop windows, walking and walking and constantly looking into windows, and finally he enters the shop and comes out of the shop again, this pleasing, polished person, I think, this refreshing person in the brisk Brussels morning, and you walk behind him and watch him. Suddenly this person falls to the ground, is dead; you see that he is dead and now you watch the other people, those who gather around the dead man and those who pay no attention at all to the dead man, and so forth . . . and you walk on. The newspapers," the prince said, "are my only distraction for weeks. For weeks I lead my life only in the newspapers. I enter the newspapers, enter the world. If my newspapers were to be taken away from me from one day to the next, I would stop existing," he said. "No better air than newspaper air, I often tell myself. Surrounded by this mountain air, Doctor, I prefer above all to breathe newspaper air. The victim of newspaper madness, I lose control of Hochgobernitz for weeks on end. The newspapers read like familiar fairy tales," the prince said. "They are often the only way I can possibly exist here. When, for example, I walk along through the mountain forests, I always have a partner who walks with me, a subject that preoccupies me, one suitable to the circumstances. No one can see him, but he is enslaved to me. I have never had a better interlocutor than myself. More and more," the prince said, "what Hochgobernitz is has already receded into the background. When I talk with anybody, no matter whom, I am always asking myself: What does this person *want*? What comes from people no longer interests me. In the autumn I think that the coming winter will put everything to rights, in the winter, the coming spring, in the spring, the coming summer, and so on. That is all. In reality nothing happens any more. I talk to myself. I am old. Have you brought me my pills? Isn't it very strenuous for you to come up here to me? To come up to me *through the gorge*? What is your son doing? It is months since I have been in Leoben. What is more, I no longer have the desire to observe people and consider everything they touch, have to touch, as artificial creations. I have already exhausted myself in contemplation. One exhausts oneself very rapidly in contemplation. Suddenly," the prince said, "I feel that I am rotting, rotting at a fantastic speed; I hear myself rotting, I hear it and want to get away from the place which I suddenly become aware of as the site of decay; but it is too late. I am no longer able to call out my name. I want to call out my name and choke over it. I look down upon myself from high above and observe: You are no longer anything. The fact is," the prince said, "in many dreams I am walking through an endless hall toward an audience which is the most important audience of my life. Since the hall I am walking through is a high, dizzying hall, an infinite hall, the audience is not possible, and because the hall is an infinite hall it is not possible for me to find out *who* is supposed to receive me in audience. I want to know who (or what) is receiving me, will receive me, but I walk and walk and walk and do not find out. There are times when I tell myself: You have nothing left but hopelessness and you must be content with that. Every day you picture hopelessness differently, I tell myself, and you stick out your tongue at it, so that you can see it laugh. Nature is, as you may know, a monstrous universal surrealism. But in fact," the prince said, "whoever is listening to something you are talking about approaches only as far as its outermost boundary. Our whole life is nothing but an approach to the outermost boundaries of life. Suddenly," he said, "a philosophical mood comes over a group which is the most ordinary group imaginable, and as a result this utterly ordinary group becomes still more ordinary. Geniuses dream only of their genius," the prince said, "stimulated by other geniuses who dream their geniuses. Or," he said, "is it possible that for me everything has already become music? I more and more have the impression that I have been turned over to a supreme court; there are always jurymen standing around me, but I don't know *who* they are. This is why I bow from time to time. I do not expect a lenient sentence. But still the death penalty seems to me a ridiculous sentence for living! I am disturbed to discover," the prince said, "that in the library I keep taking from the shelves more and more of the books that my father also read. Now many of my father's traits are awakening in me."

We had sat down on the only bench, installed on the outer wall of the castle. "The parents are perfected in the children," Prince Saurau said. Then he added, as if peering through the darkness: "There are cities in which I should like to live a long time, for years, decades, and others that I cannot bear for even the shortest time. London," he said, "is the only city in which I should like to live a lifetime. In London I could have developed in the most useful way. Unlike my son, I would have developed in London. In London I spent the happiest period of my life. Paris I fear. Paris irritates me. London calms me. Paris is nervous, London tranquil. I could have stuck it out in Hamburg for a few years, but in Vienna only for a few hours. But I do not know Stockholm, nor Marseilles, nor Lisbon. Cities that I would surely like. I am fond of Rome. Of Warsaw. But I would want to live a long time, the longest time, only in London. I am a person who was absolutely made for London but has been incarcerated in Hochgobernitz. I have always felt Hochgobernitz to be an absolutely deadly prison to me. That does not mean that I don't love Hochgobernitz. I don't love London, you know. I would like to be in London, would like to have spent my life there, but I don't love it. Hochgobernitz I love and I feel it to be a lifelong prison. Calculating machines, that is all human beings are. We calculate, we virtually always think in figures. We are born into a numerical system and one day are hurled out of it, into the universe, into nothingness. If we talk with a person for a while," the prince said, "we are alarmed because we become aware that we are talking with a calculating machine. The world is more and more merely a computer. It does us no good if we are indifferent; we are always locked up in everything and can no longer get out."

He said: "Because my daughters are like my sisters, my

daughters will some day be my sisters. I have always been deceived by everybody. *Le silence éternel de ces espaces infinis m'effraye . . . ,*" he said. "Everything I do not hold in my hand is taken away from me. If my son sells Hochgobernitz, he is lost."

My father said: "But I don't believe your son will sell Hochgobernitz."

The prince said: "He will not sell it, he'll liquidate it. Horrible," he said. "In the morning they are all afraid of being spoken to. I too am afraid of being spoken to in the morning, of being spoken to first. We hear each other as we are getting up and washing and dressing, but we are afraid of having to look at one another. Suddenly we speak to one another and are shattered. Shattered for the entire day. In this shattered state we breakfast, discuss matters concerning Hochgobernitz, the business, the people, possibilities for entertainment, proposals for meals. How we can keep warm in winter or cooler in summer. We talk about tiepins, shoe rags, travel plans. The daily routine at Hochgobernitz has always been depressing. My son is afraid of returning into this depression. Is he a revolutionary? I often ask myself. Is he a geneapolitical visionary? He apparently realizes that everything here is exhausted. Drained. From this vantage point," the prince said, "I can see everything if I make the effort, but I no longer have any desire to make an effort. I have lost the desire for any kind of effort. But on some days, without my even trying, the atmosphere is completely transparent as it could be interpenetrated by all possible qualities, and I enjoy that. Yes, I enjoy that. The great lucidity. But this condition, too, in the nature of things soon terminates in unbearableness. Everything terminates in unbearableness. I cannot bear anything; I am dead. It is quite simple: You can no longer endure things, and so that's the end. Of everything. The only force that exists, as you well know, is the force of imagination. Everything is imagined. But imagining is strenuous, is fatal. Wednesday afternoon," the prince said, "I imagine it is Wednesday afternoon, my son is in Hochgobernitz, keeping to his room. We have taken a long walk and are tired and have lain down, each in his own room. On this walk each of us inwardly worked over the subject he is most personally concerned with. No matter what we talked about, no matter what we thought, we do not understand each other. During supper, which the women cooked and served, we return to the topics of our walk. We see that nothing but age separates us. Outside it is a warm summer evening and I propose to my son that we go out again on the walls. Let us use the evening, I say, let us walk. We all go out, including the women. In the yard and then on the walls we all enjoy the combination of setting sun, walls, nature. Then darkness comes and we decide to walk down into the darkness, going as far as the gorge, past the Krainers'. We surrender ourselves to the darkness. We have surrendered ourselves to the darkness as to a science, I say. My son says: A natural science. I say: A political science. The darkness is a political science. We all wish that this summer evening would not end. We are happy. All of us are happy. I don't understand it. I often have the feeling that I may be dead the moment I leave my body to its own devices." He went on to speak of the admiration for a person that we generate in ourselves. Suddenly that person can brutally destroy our admiration by suddenly becoming, in our very presence, and simultaneously inside us, the very thing he consistently and in reality *is*. Ultimately such a discovery destroys everything, the prince said. "The truth is, all we hear in this world is: That is good, that is not good, this man is thus and so, and so on. . . . How often we hear: *He* has a keen mind, *he* hasn't, *he* speaks French fluently, *he* doesn't, *he* is materialistic, *he* isn't, *he* is a Communist, *he* isn't, *he* is poetic, *he* isn't, *he* is rich, *he* isn't. Disgusting! You know," the prince said, "in the lower classes of the population only a very small vocabulary appears, when the lower classes of the population talk at all, while in the higher classes the whole vocabulary appears, even when it is not used but repressed. And there is something else that is unbearable," he said. "The composers of symphonies always have symphonies on their minds, writers always have writing, builders always building, circus dancers always circus dancing—it's unendurable. All my life I've always been afraid, *all* my life, of suffocating from the stench of the world," he said. "That poverty is always poverty as wealth is always wealth—that is frightful. And all my life I have been saying: I want to be here or I want to be there and I am unhappy. Why? But it is also foolish to ask this question, it is impermissible. We always talk as if we had long ago discussed everything. And in fact, Doctor, everything has been said. But men go on talking, they talk on and on about their disgust whenever they talk about their destiny. And the philosophers too, Doctor, are always leading us through a museum that we already know inside and out; everything about this museum is familiar to us down to the smallest details. And it is a stinking museum that we are led into by the philosophers as soon as we occupy ourselves with their philosophies. The claim made for all philosophies is that they have opened a window and let air into the mu-

seum, fresh air, fresh air, Doctor. But the truth is that since
Kant not a single one has succeeded in airing the museum,
not a single one, I assure you. Ever since Kant the world has
been an unaired world! And science imitates philosophy; it
takes well-known bits of madness and arranges it in new patterns. We live by little surprises that we thoughtfully con-
trive for ourselves—isn't that pitiable? To think that I can
say *yes,* but that I can also say *no* to everything. People are
always standing on a point at which it is meaningless to be.
And nothing practical exists any more, nothing but theory.
In music we hear what we feel. Truth is tradition, not the
truth. I have never been able," the prince said, "to amuse
myself, never been able to entertain myself. Literalness has
always annihilated everything for me. Everything is always
annihilated by literalness. And we cannot help being born
into literalness. When we open our mouths, we kill a reputation; we simultaneously kill a reputation and kill ourselves.
But if we do not open our mouths we are soon crazy, insane,
there is nothing left of us. In dialogue, in monologue, we
draw everything more and more strenuously out of the darkness and cite it as proof; we exist only in proofs, you know,
and then we lose it again in the darkness. But only now and
then do we notice the real coarseness of life in dialogue. In
dialogue we bring the dead to life and kill the living. We
exploit this playacting until nothing is left of us but playacting. When I am in the library," the prince said, "everybody
thinks I am busy with books because I am in the library, or at
least busy with atlases, at least with printed paper. But in
reality I have not read a book for years and stopped studying
atlases, and I stay in the library only to be inside myself. The
world is more and more being used up by us; we use up the

world more than the world uses us up. My dear Doctor, what I am telling you now is a *natural history*. The incidents are always different. My life is always a different life, just as yours is, just as your son's is, as my son's is, and so on. . . . But if I am asked, though I am not asked, what kind of life my life is, I say: *My life. Consistent existences!* I say. That will arouse laughter. Contempt. General disapproval. I am constantly afraid of being asked what kind of life my life is, although I know that not a soul will ever ask me what kind of life my life is. This question cannot be put to me. This question is always asked only in order not to have to ask it, you see. Yes," the prince said, "I am growing more and more aware of causes; more and more I am growing old. And whenever I think, and therefore think of people, at bottom I always feel their weakness as a weakness that presses strongly upon me. There are, for example, periods in which I write no letters. I do not write to my son either. To no one. I conduct no correspondence; I am utterly unable to get in touch with anyone. Then again I write letters, postcards, day and night, continually, and in these letters and cards I say nothing but that I do not want to write either letters or cards and do not want to be in touch with anyone. If I am out in the open," he said, "I think that it is better not to be out in the open; if I am not in the open, I think I must be in the open. Such thoughts are aging me, are killing me."

I had wanted to go into the castle to see the inside, but the prince had no intention of terminating his "walk" for any reason whatsoever. Usually he and my father walk on the outer or the inner walls for several hours, and my father is always the prince's auditor. On this day my father wanted to be home early in the evening; he had given appointments to patients who, I thought, had probably been waiting for a very long time in his consulting room. But the prince held us. It was impossible for my father to leave. I myself, however, took the greatest interest in what the prince was saying. Moreover, it was not cold that evening. On the contrary, we could easily have taken off our jackets. But in the prince's presence I did not want to take off my jacket.

"Freedom encloses my mind like a suit of armor," the prince said, "the complete freedom that I have and that is stifling me. I am so constructed as to be entirely against reality," he said. "Most of the time I find my consolation, laugh if you like, Doctor, in inconsolability. If I am alone I feel like being with people; if I am with people I feel like being alone. I go to the greatest pains to understand others as though they were myself and I am utterly unable to understand any mind but my own. Fundamentally I am impoverished. It is quite possible that I am dying from the madnesses of others, from the illnesses of others, not from my own madnesses, not from my own illnesses, or at least not *only* from my own, not *only* from those of others. You see, Doctor, nature takes up all my thoughts and I am suffocating from having all my thoughts taken up by nature. Reality always presents itself to me as a ghastly procession of every possible concept. Theatrical effects, I always think; trying to escape from thinking, I am always thinking. For of course we are all condemned to thinking that nothing at all is actually real. Let us try it philosophically, the early centuries say; let us try it practically, the later centuries say; let us try it practically philosophically, nature says. And of late," the prince said, "people believe that *progress* is a matter of *mathematical cumulation*. No matter how we look at things, we can *feel* that the tendency is directed entirely toward death. Our teachers are dead and by always dying very early have escaped from responsibility. Our teachers have left us alone. There are no future teachers and the ones of the past are dead. You can see that everything about many people (and everything in them) is pure theory, while others are the products of neither theory nor practice. Then what? But no human being ever has the possibility of being *practical*. We live by the assumption that problems are insoluble at night, soluble by day. That makes philosophizing possible. If we start to think about how we walk, it is soon no longer possible to walk," he said. "If we start to think about how we philosophize, it is soon no longer possible for us to philosophize. And if we start to think about how we exist, we disintegrate ourselves in the briefest time. We can also draw a boundary through a person any way we please," the prince said. "We can then enter this person from one side of the boundary or the other and not cross the boundary and then go out of him again. Cultures," the prince said, "make exorbitant demands upon us. The oldest cultures the greatest demands. But what destroys us is our own culture. Just as what destroys us is our own religions, though we assert that it is nature doing it. What is needed," the prince said, "is for us to destroy the image of the world, no matter what it is like. We must always destroy all images. Reason," he said, "is dictatorial. There is no such thing as republican reason. The thinking man always finds himself in a gigantic orphanage in which people are continually proving to him that he has no parents. We all have no parents; we are never lonely but always alone. For a long time now we have been forming a world foreign legion of the mind, all of us together. And knowing that we cannot exist without being condemned, what we wish for ourselves is a constant, strict tribunal which we always understand and therefore tolerate. We always approach ourselves as if we were character traits, until we grow tired. Women naturally are not so adroit in their command of this technique. Would it be possible," the prince said, "that the air here is metaphysical air?"

My father did not answer.

"Let us continue," the prince said. "What we inhale is nothing but figures and numbers; we only assume it is nature. To us every object is one that has the form of the world, that leads back to the world's history, no matter what the object. Even the concepts that enable us to understand it have the form of the world for us, both the inner and the outer form of the world. We have not yet overcome the world in our thinking. But we make more progress in our thinking when it leaves the world completely behind. At any moment we must be prepared to jettison all concepts. Childhood," he said, "is not a foundation; therefore it is deadly. Just as I often used to leave Hochgobernitz and leave everything connected with it in charge of a steward, so I now frequently leave my brain and place it in charge of a steward. Every situation," he said, "is always *at the given instant* a political fatality. At any moment my consciousness is always completely categorical, hypothetical, disjunctive. It may well be that sharks actually fly through the air, over the woods, since nothing is fantastic, you know. . . . In all letters which say not a word about it," the prince said, "I always read the writer's bitterness at his fate. I see him communicating on the surface though he remains deep under the surface of his despair; I see his misled self misleading others, and so on. . . .

Slowly the stars, all the heavenly bodies [we could not see any], are becoming the symbols we have always regarded them as being. In that way we give ourselves the illusion of a creator. The intellect, Doctor, is nonlogical. Rescue lies in the place we do not go to because we cannot turn back. The greater the difficulties the more I enjoy living—I have often run this sentence through my brain and polished it for whole nights. Because we are determining the object by imagination, we think we are having experiences. But in reality the phenomena which we make our premises are impossible. We have an imaginary consciousness with which we must make do. It is poetry, because rationally we are aloof from reality. Once we become aware of the complex of problems relating to our existence, we think we are philosophical. We are constantly contaminated by whatever we touch; therefore we are always contaminated by everything. Our life, which is not nature, is one great contamination. In bad weather (visibility is bad) we are warned against climbing high peaks, let alone the highest. Moreover," the prince said, "we are fatigued when speculation has fatigued us. Of course everyone is constantly protecting himself by saying: I don't belong there! And he has every right to do so. I too am continually saying that I don't belong there, don't belong anywhere. But all together we are really accidental. We tire quickly whenever we don't tell lies. The foundations are in the earth, we feel, but we do not add the thought: *in the lower strata,* and we are afraid. Are we always asking too much of others?" the prince asked. "No," he answered himself, "I think not. I confront a person and I think: What are you thinking? Can I, I ask myself, go along with you inside your brain for a little? The answer is: No! We cannot go along with someone inside the brain. We force ourselves not to perceive our own abyss. But all our lives we are looking (without perceiving) down into our physical as well as psychic chasm. Our illnesses systematically destroy our lives, just as an increasingly defective orthography destroys itself." The prince said: "Everybody is continually discussing things with himself and saying: I do not exist. Every concept contains within itself an infinite number of concepts. I have always had the need, from my earliest childhood on, to enter into my fantasies, and I always have gone far into my fantasies, farther than those I have taken along with me into my fantasies, such as my sisters, for example, or my daughters, or my son. Just as they do not dare to enter infinitely deep into reality, they also do no dare enter infinitely deep into fantasies, into the realm of fantasy. We talk about sicknesses a great deal," the prince said, "about death and man's fixation on sickness and death, because we cannot really grasp sickness and death and fixation on sickness and death. Why should we sacrifice ourselves to the external spectacle, to an external act on the surface of life? Why should we so senselessly humble ourselves if we are made for the inner spectacle and all that? The mystic element in us leads directly into the allegories of the intellect: We are desperate. Yesterday," the prince said, "I was asked where Hochgobernitz is actually situated. Is it situated east or west? I was asked. I promptly answered: East! And I said: Naturally to the east. But on the way home —I was in the gorge at the time—I thought that I should have said: West. Naturally to the west. The listener is always told what he knows but does not understand," Prince Saurau said. "But we understand a great deal that we do not know. Of course, Doctor, we must do something to counteract our inborn weaknesses. Thus in regard to my son, I wonder what a man should do when nature has given him a talent that is undoubtedly unusual, although political. Especially when this man reveres his father, as he alleges, and idealizes his mother (not because she is dead!). The parents think they can expect their son to live a proper though not necessarily extraordinary life. I also can expect that, I think. Here you have your education: a young man studying in London and becoming an ecstatic visionary who only feels comfortable abroad. . . . A man wearing himself out, living in his political categories and thereby growing more and more remote from me, already a dubious character who for long periods does not answer my letters at all, and then sends only the tersest replies. I accept this son! All these letters my son writes me," the prince said, "are in reality not letters at all. They are mere signs my son has posted all around him, like: *No entry!* These letters, which give no answers whatsoever to all my questions, come from the stinking atmosphere of his room in London. My son, a scholar gone to seed, investigating something that was investigated long ago—the masses, for example. Nobody is interested in them any more. The masses no longer interest anybody because the masses have already come to power. And this son, I think, sits in England and never lets it cross his mind that he has a great guilt to atone for. . . . My son's existence seems to me a dull drifting in all the fields of knowledge. In that existence, decency gets short shrift. In my relationship with my son I have never had the pleasure of a regular correspondence, never. Actually he writes only for money, that is all. He does not care a damn that we are going to pieces here. That our lives are chained to Hochgobernitz. What he writes me are ex-

tracts from a piece of human hackwork which prove to me
that he is uselessly squandering both his gifts and my money.
I see more and more clearly that he has followed in the foot-
prints of the mass madness of mass politics. And that madness is not so ridiculous that it may not yet, in the future,
destroy everything. We have all," the prince said, "suffered
frightfully because of my son. But of course he can do as he
pleases. The sciences," the prince said, "can be regarded as a
kind of landscape in which all the seasons occur at once.
Our republic," he said, "constitutes a legal system based
on all possible vulgarities. Every administration ends in
incompetence. We sleep and dream of a world which has
been engendered by several other minds along with our own,
and we are astonished at it because we cannot know that we
are not always ourselves. Now and then we find a person,
more often in the city than in the country, in whose face we
can detect absolutely nothing that causes us pain. And we
cannot say that the person is stupid. I often pace back and
forth in the library thinking that the others are thinking that
I am pacing thoughtfully back and forth in the library,
whereas I am pacing back and forth in the library *without a
thought*. Just as children often pretend to be sleeping or dead
in order to frighten their parents, I pretend to be thoughtful.
During a conversation," the prince said, "we are often reassured by the supposition that our interlocutor's world is just
one fatal element higher or deeper than our own. We are
quite capable of visually penetrating a thing simultaneously
along its infinite breadth and along its infinite length. In letters we always report to others what seems important to us.
We often mention details for the sole purpose of describing
the path by which we ourselves are moving toward our end;

we trust another person who is traversing the same path. In the spectacle we are mounting we do not permit certain unpleasant characters to appear; should they force their way into our spectacle, we chase them out. If we were fully conscious of the mechanical aspects of our bodies, we could no longer breathe. Of late," he said, "I more and more see through people, seeing each as a mechanism, and I always detect the places where mechanical failure will (must) first occur. And I see quite clearly that I am the one who keeps all these mechanisms going. At first we go into cities to visit many people," he said. "Some that we know, others we don't know. We think we have to visit them—that is why we have gone into the cities in the first place. We try by means of human contacts to spread ourselves out over whole cities and ultimately over the whole world. But later," he said, "we go into cities in order not to visit anyone any longer, in order to hide better, to concentrate better on ourselves; we go into cities in order to disappear among the masses. I often dream extravagantly of those cities in which I can disappear, and so die away. Thought," the prince said, "is always represented as a building inhabitable for shorter or longer periods. It is generally pictured as an *intellectual edifice* in which everybody, the philosophers and their followers, can go in and out with more or less excitement. But thought cannot be represented. To me my thought is: Velocities that I cannot see." The prince said: "My sisters, like myself, were begotten unintentionally. My father often tried to convince me of the opposite; so did my mother. At such times I would suddenly feel frightened of them both.

"The shattering thing," he said, "is not the ugliness of people but their lack of judgment. I often walk for hours through the woods with my elder sister without saying a word to her. She does not notice that all the time we are walking through the woods without a word we are talking *only about her*. Her boredom is the very opposite of my boredom: the attempt to penetrate into a subject (marriage, philosophical speculation, etc.) while simultaneously trying to get out of this subject. In the past," the prince said, "I always had good relationships with people at first; now the first relationship is always a bad one. It is less strenuous to move from an initially bad relationship to a good one than vice versa, from an initially good one to a bad one. If you listen closely," the prince said, "what is told to you, played for you, is always your own story, adjusted to your rhythm. You can make this observation everywhere, no matter where, especially when traveling, at railroad stations, in waiting rooms. You are reading the newspaper and can feel the way your sickness, which is in the newspaper, in every line you read, is weakening, dominating, killing you. If we always moved in a single direction," the prince said, "we would be inside nature in the most natural way. I have often been asked why I do not keep a dog. Why there is no dog at Hochgobernitz. I always answer: *Because there is no dog here*. Darkness depends entirely on geometry. We should always look straight at the geometry of things, on which everything depends. What is ridiculous about human beings, Doctor," the prince said, "is actually *their total incapacity to be ridiculous*. I have never yet seen a ridiculous person, although everything *is* ridiculous about most of the people I see. In this house," he said, "everything makes a reasonable impression, and I have never heard anyone speak of this house as anything but a reasonable house, but in fact there is not the slightest trace of

reason in this house. Just as there is not, cannot be, the slightest trace of reason in most of the people whom we meet and
call reasonable. Hochgobernitz is altogether reasonable, but
without the slightest trace of reason. For decades I have tried
to plant trees everywhere, wherever I wanted some. As you
can see, I have planted hundreds, thousands, hundreds of
thousands of trees. Now I am no longer planting trees; now
I merely look at the hundreds of thousands of trees I have
planted. I regard them. There is no satisfaction in merely
looking. All roads are roads laid out by men. In your best
moments you speak a language that everybody understands,"
the prince said, "but nobody understands you. The resem-
blances to myself (to everything) often go so far that I no
longer know whether I am there (where I cannot be) or
here, where I no longer am. Faces grow old, as does the vul-
garity or refinement in them," he said. "I hear the strangest
birds in the night; although I know what kind of birds they
are, they become totally different at night. Outside the window, circling over Hochgobernitz, they are different. If I
hold these birds in my hand they are birds everybody knows.
My relationship to animals is such that I make them speak
human language, a newly emotional language, and they
practice human thinking. I ascribe philosophical meaning to
animals, and feel that they are very close to commanding the
grammar of nature perfectly, for which reason I am also
*afraid* of animals. The intellectual always thinks he has to
take Nature under his protection, although he is completely
dominated by her. Last night, in my dream, travelers informed me that in the midst of their journey all speed limits
were temporarily abolished, with the result that anything
was possible. That moment *existed*. Life is exactly as long as

needed for preparation for death. We talk to a person hundreds, thousands of miles away without his knowing we are talking to him. We ask questions in his stead. We answer for him. If we meet him, it seems to us that he actually had the conversation with us, the conversation that has moved us even farther apart. I often speak in such a way as to leave my interlocutor plenty of time for reflection, for talking with himself." He said: "Higher society regards lower society as useful, but the lower thinks of the higher as useless." Then the prince said: "People or rather each person by himself, can very well be viewed as a novel serialized in a daily newspaper which is printed by nature. In the editorial office, however, a horrible arbitrariness prevails, and as we see, the world daily looks forward to that arbitrariness with great eagerness. And the writers," the prince said, "make use of the truth which is useless to the philosophers."

He could explain the whole vicinity to us even in the darkness, the prince said after we had been walking slowly on the outer wall for a long time. "But whatever appeal it might have would be for myself alone. Therefore I won't explain the vicinity to you. The darkness alone makes it possible, you know, that we are *walking* where we are walking right here and now," he said. And then: "I often hear sounds that announce my son is coming, and I ask his sisters or my sisters whether they have also heard them. I heard them clearly. They do not hear them. I go to the window repeatedly and look out to see whether he is coming. I know that he will not be arriving for four or five hours, but I have already been looking out the window for the longest while. I hear him coming daily. Coming toward me daily, while I am more and more disappointed by him. For years now I have also seen my death distinctly before me. And as actual dying gradually emerges from imaginary dying, so the actual approach of my son gradually emerges from his imaginary approach. For hours I look at the quiet that prevails here. I know that this quiet has always prevailed; it is a completely unchanged quiet which has changed me, is changing me, is changing us all. Time, doctor, is quiet even in the face of nature. Once," the prince said, "I gradually turned all the clocks in Hochgobernitz back an hour every day, until we in Hochgobernitz were suddenly three days behind. I actually could have turned the clocks in Hochgobernitz back by several days, weeks, years. I had fun with that. Anyone who lives a little longer every day, if only a few minutes, at the end has saved up a whole lifetime," the prince said. "I have a habit you know, of taking all the pictures in Hochgobernitz down from the walls once a week and changing their places according to a system that I alone know, *four ahead, two back*, then again *six ahead, eight back*. All through the years up to the present day I have kept up this custom. Whenever my sisters or my daughters see me at that, I *seem* crazy to them. Perfidious mockery of perfidy," the prince said, "that is what we have in the never-changing observational material at the disposal of all of us here in Hochgobernitz. When I think of the many costume parties, masked balls, garden festivals, pavilion festivals, and plays that we have already given, seen here! Of the thousands of people who have come up and gone down again! Sometimes I hear them arriving, driving away, turning up, going down; I see them in the rhythm of my old age. I hear them laughing. I hear them in their laughter, fading away. The laughter up here is plainly something primordially human," the prince said. "Hochgobernitz as a center of pure entertainment," he said, "of magic acts. In the past the most famous magicians showed their turns here, the most famous singers sang, the most famous actors acted, the most famous writers read from their works, the most famous philosophers philosophized. Here, at one time or another the most famous of all virtuosi assembled. The virtuosi of the world met here to take leave of one another. Here," the prince said, "everything was once always the most costly, the most impressive, the most astonishing. At certain times all the languages in the world were spoken here. Hochgobernitz as a climactic point of its history in history," the prince said. "The torment is inside my body like a second body, inside my whole body like a second whole body. I dream of my amazing studies, all of which I have given up, for I no longer study at all, you know. I always pace back and forth here dreaming of my abandoned studies, of the life I have given up. Back and forth independently in this mountainous prison. What is tradition if not a perfectly acted but unbearable comedy which because it has become so incomprehensible makes our laughter freeze, in this atmosphere that makes us freeze? A play is acted here, everything is frozen hard here, and so on. What dominates this play are frozen states of mind, fantasies, philosophical tenets, idiocies, a masked-ball madness petrified at its climax. Passing by these walks, walking on these walls," the prince said, "I hear the cracks enlarging, see the complete collapse of the world's imagination impending. Whatever is very closely related to me repels me, not what is perfectly familiar to me. The quiet spreads in my head and is on the point of shattering it. I hear the way those who know all about it speak about me in significant tones, try to fool me with their show of concern. But

my weakness has always been my strength; I am what I am
out of weakness. When I dream, I first direct my attention to
the whole world and only then to the dream I am dreaming
by examining myself in a strictly scientific spirit. The feeling
that permits a person to elude death for a longer or shorter
period—we have it often—has for me become crudely stapled
together with long sentences, comprehensible or incomprehensible ones. In books I have always discovered how unhappy I am, how callous, how insanely irresponsible, how
sensitive, how superfluous. Think of a whole nation," the
prince said, "in centuries of unconsciousness, making history
in this unconsciousness! Never have I been so clearly aware
of this state as I am now. The underlying meaning of several
objects taken together is not necessarily revealed to us when
the underlying meaning of each of those objects is revealed
to us. There you have the problem of *history*. I have earned
the right to an idea when I have worked (metaphysically)
all my life for this idea, when I have lived for it, existed for it,
been mistreated and denounced for it. In the nerves, Doctor,
the relationships which result in total chaos are touched on.
Another man may now, at this season and in this century, be
walking on the wall, alternating between the inner and the
outer wall, just like us (perhaps that man is the doctor?), in
keeping with the makeup of his mind, and he may say exactly as I do: *I have nothing. Nothing.* It does not hurt me, it
merely torments me. Everything, I think, is only a geometry
of bickerings, doubts, sufferings, ultimately torments," the
prince said. "I stand at the window and see myself in the
yard, on the inner wall. While I observe myself I understand
myself, I do not understand myself. I am four years old, I am
forty years old. I play with myself, I *play,* I consider, I think.

Someone calls me; it is a summer evening, my grandmother calls me, my grandfather, my mother, my father. They call me. Standing at the window I see, one after the other, my grandfather, my grandmother, my father, my mother, my wife. The seasons change continually while I stand at the window. They all call me. My father has on his winter suit, grandfather his winter coat, my grandmother her sheepskin coat, my mother her riding habit. I do not see my wife, I hear her but do not see her. For a whole hour I stand at the window and observe the scenery, which lies far back, very far in the background, and which I change according to my taste and by exercise of my own will. If I suddenly call out into it, this scenery dissolves," the prince said. "I close the window, turn away from the scenery; it goes on. I forget it and it goes on. Without my constantly changing it, irritating it. Now this scenery is utterly without irritation. It often happens," the prince said, "that I hear my wife. She very distinctly speaks sentences she spoke during her lifetime, but I cannot *see* her. For brief moments I think she is here; I turn around, but see nothing. My father-in-law, her father, frequently appeared in Hochgobernitz after his death; she met him, was able to see him and talk with him. But I only hear my wife, never see her. When she speaks I have the impression that the language she speaks has changed in the interval since her death, although she says the same things as she did in her lifetime. Her language, I think, is still aging while herself is dead. Dead? She certainly is not one of those people who are completely dead when they are dead; she has died, but is not dead. But I am no longer writing such a study, although for a long time I wanted to do one, had in mind a study which describes this process. I no longer have any studies in mind. I hear my wife behind me, I turn around, she is not there, I call after her, out into the corridor, down into the vestibule, into all the upper and lower rooms. My sisters think me crazy, my daughters likewise think me crazy. I ought to go back to my room, they say. Who gives them the right to order me to my room? But I do not allow myself to challenge them and go to my room at once. My wife's father appeared to her frequently after his death, everywhere in Hochgobernitz; she not only saw him but was able to *experience* him," the prince said. "Whenever I myself have invited guests," he said, "for years I have had the feeling that I have invited enemies. Enemies of my mind above all. They think they can risk entering a league with my sisters and my daughters. I have always thought that I myself am paying for the impertinence of all my guests, first covert, then overt, in promptly taking the side of the women. I pay for everything that irritates me. And so I stopped inviting anyone to Hochgobernitz. Everybody dreaded my lectures," the prince said. "It was my habit to deliver a matutinal address at breakfast, to place a philosophical question on the table. Political matters interested me above all; for decades they started me going when I awakened, or in fact before I had really awakened. Whenever I met someone, no matter where, someone suitable, that is, I began talking politics. And I defended my views at once even before I had heard the other person express his views, because I knew them before he expressed them. Nobody needs to open his mouth for me to know what his politics are. I feel that in advance, I feel it at once. Such and such a person has such and such politics in his head, I always thought whenever I met someone. I thought that about everybody all my life. In general everyone was and is afraid that I will address him. As you know I despise whatever is without effort. That is my highest principle, the only one I have. I always demand the utmost. But people are afraid of the utmost. I have almost always had nothing but domestic *enemies*. I am cold, I say to my sisters, and my sisters bring me my pullover. I say again, I am cold, and they bring me my overcoat, and I say again, I am cold, and they bring my fur boots and fur hood, and then I begin to undress and to feel better. I am saved, I think, I am no longer cold, I am completely naked, I am no longer cold, and that disturbs them. The cold that prevails here in Hochgobernitz has always had the greatest influence. It has always influenced everybody here. The cold in conjunction with the dampness of the old walls. Even in my most complicated thoughts I have always felt this cold and this dampness, always noted it. Yes," he said, "possibly everything about me could be attributed to the cold and dampness. There are entirely different characters in the world, who are completely independent of one another and who yet are constantly being formed by climatic conditions. You can say of many of them that they grew up in a dry, a damp, a warm, or a cold house. Your home was cold, you could say to many, and to many others: You come from a dry home. And so on. People's characters adjust to the climate; the climate changes them to accord with it. There are philosophies that could not arise in dry and others that could not arise in damp houses. There are concatenations of ideas which have their origin in cold walls. We assume the spirit of the walls that surround us. I often see groups of people and think: This group comes from a damp region, this from a dry one. Some come from a completely parched area. In the course of the centuries exter-

nal nature has completely permeated Hochgobernitz. I also
sleep *in* this nature, I frequently think; I sleep *in* the dampness and cold typical of Hochgobernitz. And so I think in
this dampness and cold. Hochgobernitz is the proof that a
building can destroy people who are completely at its mercy.
But it does not do any good to leave the building that will
destroy you, to go away from Hochgobernitz for example. It
encloses you wherever you go. Whether you go to London or
Paris, it crushes you. Traveling far away has no point. Even
in New York I always had the feeling that Hochgobernitz
was crushing me, not New York. But it is much better to be
crushed by Hochgobernitz in Hochgobernitz than in New
York. We always want to hear something even worse than
what we have inside of us," the prince said. "That is the sole
reason we listen, force ourselves to hold conversations. The
noiselessness sometimes makes everything in Hochgobernitz
so distinct," he said, "makes everything past and future into
the present. At times, when this noiselessness prevails and
when I want to, I can effortlessly identify all the voices I have
ever heard or not heard in Hochgobernitz. The violence of
external nature, which continually arises from the mind of
internal nature," the prince said, "is the quiet. In fact I once
suddenly awakened in the middle of the night and saw a
gigantic note pinned to the sky on which the word *open* was
written. My laughter awakened everyone in the house. They
rushed to the windows and saw nothing. I kept saying,
*Open! Open!* is written up there, really, *open* is actually
written up there, but they saw nothing, thought me crazy,
and I chased them back to their beds. In the nature of things
I am more and more afraid of myself," the prince said. "I am
actually frightened. I try to distract myself from this fear, but

I succeed only sporadically nowadays. What satisfaction I felt only a few years ago when I went down into the valleys, down into the gorge, into the mountain forest on fine days and into the lowland forest on rainy days. I was often happy contemplating the surface of the water at the Ache, happy at the rhythm of movement of the water itself, absorbed in poetic appreciation of the earth's surface. The lowland forest, the Ache itself, was enough to keep me from despair. And if not the Ache, if not the mountain forest or the lowland forest, then the library. Books that make for contemplation. My mind was all right, my brain all right, I was all right. Today? For years all I needed was to think of my son, of my own youth, and I would go out of my room and down to join the women. A meal with them. A conversation with them. In those days I was convinced of the proximity of infinity. Today? Everything is very far away today. Farther and farther away. Did I ever approach the explanation? Lying in bed I am ashamed of myself. Then I get up because I am hungry, go down to the women and eat something, and feel as if I am plunging into double shame, hundredfold shame. Life more and more has an ill-smelling breath. And I am afraid of someday being discovered in my feelings. My life consists of efforts not to be discovered. Have they discovered me, seen through me? I often think. Which of them has discovered, seen through me? I am the world and must also incorporate it into myself in the form of books, vast libraries," the prince said. "Absurd. While reading, no matter what I read in the past, I always had the feeling that everything was divided into two halves, into a decent and an indecent half. That is what is repulsive about reading: the division into two halves. I won't say Good and Evil, but decent, indecent. But thinking is free of this repulsiveness. In reading, one tries to ignore oneself," the prince said. "Permanent identity as consolation. An initially melancholic but then more and more tormenting kind of imagining influences us. I always tell myself that I know everything is fatal, but I act contrarily. My head is often separated from my body by the span of several centuries or millennia and absolutely an empirical *master of galvanization*. I always have fever, Doctor, but it is the kind of fever the thermometer does not show. I am a barometer that is no longer functioning. In court I once met a person I had never seen before," the prince said, "but who reminded me of all the people I have ever seen. He said he had something magnificent in store for his head. But I must not think he was going to cut it off himself. He put a knife into my hand and said: *Cut my head off, my dear fellow. I have long waited for you to turn up to cut off my head. For I have something magnificent in store for my head. Don't be afraid,* this eccentric said, *I have calculated everything in advance. It cannot go wrong. Here, cut!* He gave me three minutes. *Here,* he said, *this is the spot where I want my head cut off. I'll continue to stand, because it seems to me thoroughly undignified to have your head cut off while lying down, let alone sitting. I won't embarrass you!* the stranger said. *Incidentally, the knife is manufactured by the Christofle Company,* he said. And I actually saw the name Christofle engraved on the knife. I seized the head and cut it off. I was quite astonished at how easy it was. The head then said: You see, you had no difficulty cutting off my head. But then I see that I haven't cut off his head, and the stranger said: *You didn't seriously imagine you could cut off my head, did you? Or did you? Let us go on,* the stranger said. He was my cousin. Actually," the prince said, "I did not dream the story to its end. That was a pity."

The prince said: "We are without parents. We are orphans. That is our condition, and we shall not, Europe will not escape from this condition ever again. The question has always been, how can I expand, how solidify Hochgobernitz even more. Never before has Hochgobernitz been so utterly cut off from the world and simultaneously so dependent on the world. I am always afraid of earthquakes. It is no longer possible for me to walk without thinking about earthquakes, feeling earthquakes, future earthquakes, noises, underground noises, and at the same time noises inside my head. I have the idea," the prince said, "that we are writing letters, sending letters, and receiving letters, and that the signatures on all these letters are illegible. Who writes all these sent and received letters? I see how the catastrophe is shaping up; looking out of the window I see it shaping up noiselessly, taking place noiselessly. I am not allowed to speak of it. But the fact that I occupy the smallest room in vast Hochgobernitz is uncanny, Doctor. This room, moreover, is the dampest and coldest. Suppose I were to write an essay in my room, I think, a study bearing the simple title *My Room,* into which I would squeeze the entire world. I would squeeze the entire room into my room and into my study. No, not a study," the prince said. "The thinking man's task is more and more to remove images from his memory. His goal has been attained when there is no longer a single image in his brain. When the representational potentialities of his brain are exhausted. I bear no guilt," he said. "I often tell myself, I know I bear no guilt. Guilt? For decades I tried to communicate; as long as I have been alive nothing but the attempt to communicate has consumed me. At first I started trying to communicate with my parents, my sisters, my children. I wanted to communicate with everybody. Now I am trying to communicate with you, and with your son. Actually," the prince said, "these September nights can already be very cold. The cold comes up from below, from the gorge. It is usually ice cold here. Hochgobernitz is made of ice. People frozen into ice in Hochgobernitz. The times in which we live obviously are poor for furthering communication. At first," the prince said, "my mother thought of me as a crime against herself, later as a crime she had committed. Then I became a nuisance to her. Then she began to despise me, then to love me, to hate me, because she always felt forced to identify with me. For the parents, children are an incurable tumor which deforms them for life. I withdraw more and more into my room as a sickroom. I have always taken everything I have in this room, the food, the reading, the thinking, as if it were medicine, emotional fluids, intellectual liquids, tablets of philosophy. Being incurable is a condition that has lasted ten years. I have been conscious of this condition for that long—a nondenominational disease inherited by right of succession," the prince said. "You see, Doctor, I am putting on my jacket, and I am taking my jacket off again. I bought this jacket in Brussels, that one in London, that one in Cairo. I am putting on the Cairo jacket, taking off the London jacket, putting on the Brussels jacket, taking off the Cairo jacket. Curiosity, which costs so much money," the prince said. "Naturally I cannot leave Hochgobernitz. I always bought newspapers and without reading them, merely leafing through them, threw them away again not a hundred paces away from the newsstand where I bought them. If I were to let the newspapers I have bought in my life blow down Kärntnerstrasse as a newspaper drift, a newspaper drift like a snowdrift, Kärntnerstrasse would be completely stuffed up in no time at all; everything in Kärntnerstrasse would be smothered, half of Vienna would be smothered; people would be smothered under the newspapers I have bought in my life, could be buried and smothered; a deadly newspaper winter would descend on Vienna. I see," the prince said, "the fever of childhood in the faces of children. Childhood tires quickly; age is the recollection of childhood. Best of all to be in bed and be able to fall asleep—for a long time now that has been all I want or need. Have you properly made use of your body? I think. Of your mind? Of life? When you begin to worry about that, you're already past it. Foolish statements," the prince said. "On railroad platforms, often, I am struck by the notion of throwing myself under the train at the last moment, but in big city toilets I find I am still curious after all. Pleasure in inventing complicated, impeccable sentences. Grasping the meaning of the word *ethometer*. Grasping the helplessness of all people, but without pity. The necessity of letting everything you know freeze hard. Challenging the steward who dismissed five gravel pit workers," the prince said. "I ask: *Why?* He does not answer me. I say the gravel pit workers are not to be dismissed; it is dangerous to dismiss even a single gravel pit worker. We must not dismiss any of them, I say, but the steward dismisses the five. Instantly I feel something sinister about the gravel pits. . . . Or," the prince said, "I walk on the outer wall, right here where we are walking now, and pick up a chestnut leaf. The chestnut leaf reminds me of my mother;

as I look at it I see her. Its smell reminds me of *Measure for Measure*. I see *Measure for Measure*. *Measure for Measure* reminds me of a pair of old shoes I wore as a child, and so on. . . . We see a person and instantly pass judgment," the prince said. "This is a clever person, we say, a stupid person, a rabid person, a happy person, a cultivated, foolish, sociable, always laughing, always hopeless, always businesslike, always vulgar, always pitiable person . . . and we understand nothing. If we say, *he is a catastrophic person,* without knowing him, if we say, *he is* dead, and so on. . . . We see in a person frailties which at once make us see the frailties of the community in which we live, the frailties of all communities, the state; we feel them, we see through them, we catastrophize them. The greater the capacity for judgment, the greater the wariness. Our wariness slowly permeates everything. Even as a child my father toyed with the thought of killing himself. It cost him the greatest self-control, whenever he crossed the Ache, not to throw himself into the Ache. To hang himself. To shoot himself. This thought dominated him. Thinking in possibilities of suicide as a learned discipline subordinate to science," the prince said. "The mystical element in my thinking has almost been switched off. Isolation. Nothing has purpose," he said. "The millions of experiments," he said, "lead back to the source, if we look at them with open eyes. These experiments in the mass and in so-called untrammeled nature. Nothing is easier than to escape into the commonplace. I say something," the prince said, "and I immediately perceive the opposite of it in myself. We can persuade ourselves that we are not alone with a book, as we can persuade ourselves that we are not alone with a person. When we hire an actor, we want to be entertained; we blast him if he forgets that. We always live in the delusion (because we think it will enable us to live) that we can escape completely from at least one of the elements of nature, that for example we are able to make a revolution, to topple a king from his pinnacle, and so on. . . . The eye is often abandoned by the intellect, the intellect by the eye. Nowadays," the prince said, "we feel at ease in biblical descriptions; we have discovered the poetry of Sodom and Gomorrah and *feel* it. We are no longer fearful unto death, we *go* to death. Illnesses lead man by the shortest path to himself. Of course we must demand precision at least in our first premises. A man without a brain would be thoughtless. Our teachers have been enemies of our intellects. What does not concern us vexes us. For a long time now I have been concerned not with the idea of who will be on the moon tomorrow, but who will be the first to *travel through the earth*. The complete conversational incapacity of my wife, who could be sentimental about the whole world in regard to any single thing. Fatal diseases spreading everywhere. Always thinking in comparisons between the upper, *my,* and the lower, *their,* rooms. Habits, tendencies that have slowly consumed us all. Our impoverishment in action. In the lower rooms philosophy is no more possible than mysticism in the upper rooms. Sometimes I hear all the clocks in the house so loudly that I must get up and stop them. That requires several hours. Then I can fall asleep. Formerly, as children, we knocked on the walls to communicate with one another. Now nobody has knocked on the walls for half a century. In no time at all Hochgobernitz will be tenanted by the beetles and spiders," the prince said. "Beetles and spiders as nature's craziness, I often think. Everything is mystification," he said.

We drove rapidly home by way of Landschach. "Unrewarding cases," my father said. My sister had already gone to bed. Tomorrow, I thought, I'll go for another walk with her and talk with her. It was already eleven o'clock. My father had yet another call to make, on a butcher in Krennhof who had shot himself in the belly with the apparatus used for shooting the animals. He expected to be back before midnight. While he was gone I thought about the utter silence in which we had descended from Hochgobernitz into the gorge and then driven out of the gorge. Tomorrow your father will take you back to Leoben in the early afternoon, I thought. You need not bother to unpack your suitcase. The local constable had been waiting for my father to hear the final word on the dead wife of the innkeeper. Grössl had been arrested, he reported. I did not want to wake my sister. I sat up trying to write a long overdue letter to a friend of my uncle who has a farm near Guttaring in Carinthia. He had invited me there a long time ago. I wanted to write that I would not be coming, could not come. My studies did not allow of any interruption just now, I had written, and then tore up the letter I had begun. In bed I thought: *What did the prince say?* "Always wanting to change everything has been a constant craving with me, an outrageous desire which leads to the most painful disputes. The catastrophe begins with getting out of bed. With putting everything on a philosophical basis, with making a public display of oneself. The darkness is cold when the head is switched off." *The notebook:* "For days," the prince said, "I have been searching my pockets for my mislaid notebook. This notebook of mine contains some remarkable entries. *Underlined!* My sickness is underlining important things; there are almost nothing but underlinings in this notebook, and all these underlined sentences begin with the destruction of these sentences. . . . I have been searching my pockets for days for this notebook, and suddenly I found it downstairs in the kitchen. How has my notebook come to be in the kitchen? I ask myself. For days I have not been in the kitchen and suddenly I find my notebook in the kitchen. A horrible suspicion arises in me. I suspect that my elder sister took the notebook out of my jacket pocket and in the kitchen—I am a person altogether hostile to kitchens—surreptitiously read it through and left it lying there in the kitchen. I go to my elder sister at once and say: The terrible thing is the fact that you left my notebook lying in the kitchen, not that you have absorbed its contents! But I see that my elder sister cannot possibly have left the notebook lying in the kitchen, and go at once to my younger sister. I tell her straight to her face that it is a dastardly thing to read my notebooks, to take them out of my pockets and read them. I am afraid you have read all my notebooks, I say, but this is the first one you have left lying in the kitchen. Until now I have lived in the delusion that none of you is familiar with the contents of my notebooks, that you know nothing at all about what is in these notebooks. I force my younger sister into the office, because it seems monstrous to me that she of all persons has read this notebook. I recall immediately that in the notebook I have constantly made derogatory comments on my two sisters, but especially on the younger one. I have lived in the delusion, I say, that what I have written in my notebooks, written for decades, is completely unknown. And now I find that I am keeping my notebooks in public, I am keeping my notebooks publicly. But then I suddenly perceive that my younger sister does not even have an inkling of the existence of my notebooks, and I at once tell myself, of course such a *superficial person* as my sister has not the slightest inkling of the existence of my notebooks, of course, and I say: *None of you care about anything concerning me!* I say: *Some day you will make the most frightful discoveries in these notebooks, you will make expeditions into your atrociousness.* Just because I keep silent about everything in my daily association with you, I need not keep silent about anything in my notebooks! All my ruthlessness bursts upon you in my notebooks. Upon *you,* upon your sister, upon my daughters, upon my son, upon everybody! Then, when I am dead, I shall cast a pall over you for a long while through my notebooks, I say, and you will think back on my presence with horror, on your brother and father! In the notebooks, I say, you have actually taken form, horrible form. Well, I say, if you did not leave the notebook lying in the kitchen, *who did* leave it lying in the kitchen? And I go out of the office and look for my elder daughter. It occurs to me that *she alone* is capable of taking my notebook out of my pocket and leaving it lying in the kitchen. I go through the whole house looking for my elder daughter. First I go through the lower rooms, then the upper rooms, but I do not find my elder daughter. Probably she is hiding, I think, because she has heard about the fuss over the notebook. I call, I walk in silence, then again calling, alternatively calling and silent, through the entire house. Finally it occurs to me that she might be in the pavilion. I go into the pavilion and find her on the sofa, reading a novel. I say at once: *Where is my notebook?* Yes, I say, I found my notebook in the kitchen. *This outrageous human race, now it has actually laid impious hands on my notebooks,* I say. Probably you have been laying impious hands on my notebooks for years, I say. Possibly, I say, you have laid impious hands on all my notebooks. And probably, I say, what you have read into all my notebooks has made you turn against me with horrible cruelty. I hope, I say, that the upshot will be that you get out of Hochgobernitz, move out, move down to join your kind! But suddenly," the prince said, "I realized that my elder daughter too *could in no way be connected with the notebook*. Then my younger daughter, I think. But nobody knows where she is. *I want to know where she is!* I shout. They say she has gone to the city. To the city! I say. I go about the lower rooms thinking that when night falls I shall take all the pictures hanging there down from the walls, all of them. And all the pictures in the upper rooms also, I say. And I will hang others. *More frightful ones.* Slowly, I calm down," the prince said, "and then I hear my sisters whispering all at once. I must destroy this whispering, I think, and I go and chase them away. *No matter which of you took my notebook from my pocket and left it lying in the kitchen,* I say, *you must all suffer for it, all together.* Partners in crime, I think, the women are partners in crime. I have, I think, very expensive destroyers of my own person here in Hochgobernitz. And while I am ordering them to do a job that has to be done," the prince said, "a disgusting household job, it occurs to me that I myself left the notebook lying in the kitchen, that, sleepless as always, I went into the kitchen in the middle of the night to drink something refreshing.

"I could not fall asleep, and began writing," the prince said. "I wrote, A son studies his father and studies only how to destroy his father. And the women have always known *how.* . . . As a matter of habit," the prince said, "I still go to the office, with the punctuality which in the course of my life has so deformed me that I no longer recognize myself. *Farming, forestry,* I think. *Incompetent.* I don't have the strength to go out of the office, to leave the office once and for all, although there is no point in my being in the office. I think: Why am I staying in the office if not for purposes of farming and forestry? This thought stimulates the most sensitive parts of my brain and I take a variety of files from the shelves in order to calm myself. This procedure, my going to the office and not knowing what to do in the office, is now being repeated daily. I no longer have any relationship to the entire contents of the office," the prince said. "My son," he said, "will come back from England and destroy Hochgobernitz. The long paper comes to my mind, that draft of his. In London, it seems to me, he has entangled himself in a philosophy from which he cannot emerge other than totally deranged. Hochgobernitz will be possible for him only as a crazy Hochgobernitz. I feel that. Incidentally, my son knows nothing about farming and forestry. What my son feels to be nature is not nature. He will possibly try to sell Hochgobernitz as a whole. But there will be no takers, and so he will break it up. After my death I see Hochgobernitz as stricken with terror. Then my son will come and dissolve the tension in madness. He is my son; everything will be at his mercy. Fatal times will come then, especially for my sisters, but also for my daughters, times of utter helplessness. But probably all these creatures deserve ruthlessness more than pity. My son always regards nature as a form of literature; all his letters confirm that. My son despises me, you know, Doctor. There is no truth in his letters. His handwriting changed completely in the course of a single year. I support my son in studies repulsive to me, and he is destroying me. We, my son and I, could never have a conversation with each other. In England he has become accustomed to such short sentences, a way of talking that is painful, killing. I have raised him to be my destroyer, I think. And this man dares to write me in his last letter that I am a dilettante, that I failed to shape my life into an art. But he, as his letter proves, is shaping his life into an art, he writes. Whenever I ought to have drawn him closer to myself, he writes, I have pushed him away of my own accord. But all education is always utterly wrong," the prince said. "My son's actions have always been opposed to me. The one and only thing we have in common is our fondness for the newspapers. Oh yes," the prince said, "would you mind getting me a copy of the *Times* of September seventh and bringing it the next time you come up . . . ?"

ALSO BY THOMAS BERNHARD

---

*"A complex and unsettling novel . . . about genius and obsession . . . mirroring the thought process of a compulsive mind."* —The New York Times Book Review

### THE LOSER

Thomas Bernhard was one of the most original writers of the twentieth century. His formal innovation ranks with Beckett and Kafka, his outrageously cantankerous voice recalls Dostoevsky, but his gift for lacerating, lyrical, provocative prose is incomparably his own. One of Bernhard's most acclaimed novels, *The Loser* centers on a fictional relationship between piano virtuoso Glenn Gould and two of his fellow students who feel compelled to renounce their musical ambitions in the face of Gould's incomparable genius. One commits suicide, while the other—the obsessive, witty, and self-mocking narrator— has retreated into obscurity. Written as a monologue in one remarkable unbroken paragraph, *The Loser* is a brilliant meditation on success, failure, genius, and fame.

Fiction/Literature/1-4000-7754-0

Printed in the United States
by Baker & Taylor Publisher Services